### A Haunting Presence . . .

I woke with a start. My room was filled with that blackness that comes shortly before dawn. I was wide awake, but I felt disoriented; there was something different, something wrong. I lay quite still, staring up into the darkness, when I remembered I had left the bathroom light burning before I fell asleep. Now it was dark and there was something . . .

Dear God! I thought, and my heart lurched as fear shook me. Now I could hear it quite clearly; from somewhere nearby, out of the inky blackness came the unmistakable sound of breathing.

F. JACQUELYN HALLQUIST

# THE HOUSE ON WIFFEN COVE

A Dell Book

Published by
Dell Publishing
a division of
Bantam Doubleday Dell Publishing Group, Inc.
666 Fifth Avenue
New York, New York 10103

ISBN: 0-440-21340-1

Printed in the United States of America

Published simultaneously in Canada

January 1993

10  9  8  7  6  5  4  3  2  1

RAD

# THE HOUSE ON
# WIFFEN COVE

# ONE

Sometimes, when sleep eludes me, I lie wide-eyed, watching the shadows cast by the rising moon writhe and tremble upon the wall. And when the moon is full, even if the night air is cool, I must rise, go to the window in the alcove, stare down into the garden below me—so like that other garden. The birdbath is the same. The graveled path, washed by moonlight, is the same ribbon of silver, winding among the flower beds to disappear at length under the trees.

And sometimes, as I stand there in the darkness, I seem to hear again the muted crunch of gravel beneath stealthy boots. My heart begins to pound, and I stare fearfully into the blackness at the garden's edge. But the garden remains empty, the illusion fades. Slowly, I relax, and while I wait for the dawn, I remember. . . .

I remember the winter David and I met. How young, how eager, how full of joy we were. And we knew from that very first day that we were meant for each other—it was love at first sight—kismet. I knew it. He knew it. Everyone who saw us together knew it.

Not that David was the handsomest man I had ever known, though he was tall and lithe with the broad shoulders and tapered hips of an athlete. His dark hair was thick and unruly; his dark eyes were warm and already crinkled at the corners by his love of laughter. And just looking at him made me feel like a toasted marshmallow.

So, at the tender age of nineteen, I dropped out of the fine arts program at UCLA and married my beloved. Everyone said I was a beautiful bride, though that may have been a bit of an exaggeration. People who love you tend to do that.

I do have nice eyes—green and wide-set; but my nose, I am told, is pert, whereas my mouth is on the generous side. However, they do say happiness lends beauty, and no two people were ever happier than my David and I. Our world was filled with sunshine, the future was bright with promise. No bad dreams for us—no forebodings—no premonitions.

Nothing to prepare me for the horrors I would have to face when an automobile accident destroyed our unborn child and left David an invalid, confined forever after to a wheelchair. We had been married for eleven months.

The years that followed were difficult. That accident not only deprived David of his health, it also robbed him of his career as a geologist. No longer could he travel deserts and mountains, on foot and by horseback, searching out the earth's secrets. His body, once so strong, so vital, was made forever useless from the chest down. Overnight, the only thing we could count on was medical bills: endless, horrendous. There was insurance, of course, but it hadn't gone very far.

Nevertheless, because David needed constant care, care that would have cost more than I could ever have hoped to earn, I never sought employment outside the home. Instead, together we opened a small art boutique. We handled handcrafted jewelry and pottery, watercolors and oils by local artists, hand-painted greeting cards and postcards. David assumed responsibility for buying, marketing, and bookkeeping; I handled public relations.

We catered to the tourist trade in the small coastal town in Southern California where we had lived for most of our lives. Our business was reasonably successful, and I did supplement our income painting pet portraits. But it was a hand-to-mouth existence at best.

However, the mental and physical anguish we faced during those seven years following the accident did not diminish the love we felt for one another. Changed it, tempered it, but never diminished it. And over those seven years, because some of the avenues of communication shared by most couples had been lost to us, we developed other, less tangible ways of sharing, of understanding. So strong were those bonds, sometimes, in some inexplicable fashion, I *heard* David's thoughts as clearly as ever I heard his spoken words.

That's the way it was that day in May when the postman delivered the registered letter from Washington State. Even though I was busy in the kitchen when the doorbell rang, the sudden surge of surprise that welled up in David set my heart to beating faster too.

I dropped the apple I was peeling into the colander and hurried to the living room. "What's up?" I asked, watching as David tore a strip off one end of an official-looking envelope.

Without answering, David extracted a batch of papers, and as he skimmed the cover letter, a long low whistle confirmed his astonishment. I moved around beside his wheelchair and began to read over his shoulder.

The letter was from a lawyer in Seattle informing David that his aunt, Sylvia Belgedes, had left him a small holding on an island in the Strait of Juan de Fuca.

Suddenly, my heart began to pound. Could this be for real? I laid a hand on David's shoulder. Automatically he covered it with his own, but we just kept on reading, not speaking.

The bequest included a residence known as the House on Wiffen Cove, together with all chattels, plus approximately two acres of land. In addition, there was a small income from a trust fund, to be distributed quarterly to David or his heirs, for as long as he, or they, lived in the house.

The letter went on to explain that if David, or his heirs, did not live in the house, the law firm was directed to establish a foundation to administer the proceeds from the trust and make such use of the house and property as would most benefit the island and its inhabitants. The estate would vest in whomever was occupying the house on January 1, in the year 2000. The letter closed with the assurance that the attorney was prepared to be of assistance in any way David might deem necessary.

A map was enclosed on which someone had circled in red a tiny island called Saturday. It was located about halfway between Port Townsend, Washington, and Victoria, British Columbia. A large red arrow pointed to a spot on the western side of the island from which a small finger of land jutted out into the Strait of Juan de Fuca. Inked in beside it was the name Wiffen Cove.

David looked up at me then and we stared at each other. Momentarily speechless, I went all trembly with excitement. A house! Money! After all the years of worry and doing without; now, straight out of the blue, the prospect of a home of our own—an assured income . . .

I was afraid to believe. "Maybe we should call that attorney . . . be certain there's no mistake . . . ?"

David nodded. "Does seem too good to be true." Suddenly, he leaned his head back and flashed me a smile that momentarily masked the lines of pain that etched his still boyish face. My heart twisted in my breast, but I returned his smile.

"I really do have an Aunt Sylvia."

"You do? How come no one ever mentioned her?"

"She was Dad's kid sister . . . sort of the black sheep of the family."

"Black sheep? Why? What did she do?"

David shook his head, some of the excitement draining from his thin pale face. "I don't really know . . . got mixed up in the drug scene while she was still in high school . . . ran away and joined a commune . . . some such thing. . . ."

"Did you know her?"

"I met her once. . . ."

"What was she like?"

David shook his head. "It's been a long time. . . ." He screwed his eyes shut in an effort to recall those long ago days. Then he sighed. "I haven't thought of her in years. . . ."

I continued to press for details until David, sounding a tad annoyed, said, "Hey! I was only twelve years old. . . ." Abruptly, he brightened. "Two things I do remember: She was the prettiest woman I had ever seen, and she always smelled good!"

In the end we did call the attorney; he confirmed the validity of the bequest and indicated that probate could probably be completed within six months. Elated, we spent the ensuing hour pouring over the letter and the copy of the map, speculating, daydreaming about what we would do when we were finally ensconced in our very own home.

A month later David was dead. The doctors ascribed his death to a massive bacterial infection. . . .

There's a song Barbra Streisand sings; something about what's too painful to remember, just choose to forget. That's the way I felt; and on the day we buried David, I tried to bury all my memories, all my dreams that could never come true as well.

Now I was completely on my own. David was gone; his parents were gone; I never knew my father. He died before I was born. My mother abandoned me when I was sixteen.

Still, I was not truly alone. I did have Emma and Jerry Tuttle—they are my dearest friends in all the world and the closest thing to parents I ever knew. After my mother left, it was they who kept me off the streets and in school.

Emma and Jerry were there for me when David and I married, they had offered me their love and strength after the accident, they stood with me at David's graveside. And when the funeral was over, Emma and Jerry drove me home and sat with me for a while, offering what comfort they could. I thanked them, but begged to be left alone. I felt only tired, filled with aching emptiness, as if a huge chunk of my life had broken loose and fallen into that bottomless black hole that had suddenly yawned in the pit of my stomach.

Indeed, I think I would have fallen into that hole and drowned in my own grief had it not been for our cats: Sheba, who had spent half her life sleeping on David's knees; Clarence the clown, who loved to tease; and dainty little Cleopatra. They came to sit with me when Emma and Jerry had gone: Sheba in my lap, Clarence close beside me, while Cleo twined herself about my ankles, her purr a mellifluous song deep in her throat. Just to have them near, these creatures who had shared my love for David and his for me, to feel the silky warmth of their coats beneath my fingers, see the affection in their eyes, soothed and calmed me, brought me some measure of solace and peace.

It was late when I went to bed that night, and I lay awake tossing and turning until almost dawn, haunted by memories of what never was—what never could be now. . . . But as it always must, sleep came at last, and sleeping, I dreamed: a strange dream, a faceless dream, a dream I could not clearly recall in the morning. Yet when I woke, I knew what David wanted me to do.

From the time I was old enough to hold a brush, I had only one goal, one desire: to paint. Not just animal portraits, though that was fun. I wanted to *paint*—develop my own style, express my own feelings and insights, create something meaningful. Now, with the availability of a house and an income large enough for me to live on, the time had come. And I knew, as surely as if I had heard him speak the words, that it was what David wanted me to do.

I called the attorney in Seattle that very morning and told him that as David's heir, I still intended to take possession of the House on Wiffen Cove as soon as possible. He informed me that I would have to wait until not only Aunt Sylvia's will, but David's as well, had been through probate. Nevertheless, he felt certain everything could be settled by the first of the year. In the meantime, he assured me, money from the trust would accrue to an account, payable to me as soon as I moved into the house. It would take approximately six months for everything to be settled.

Six months. It seemed such a long time. And yet it would give me time to sell the boutique, tie up all the loose ends—to write *fini* to my life with David.

*David!* That black hole in the pit of my stomach suddenly yawned wider, deeper, threatening to swallow me up. *How could I go on without David?* I clenched my teeth and wrapped my arms tight around me in a mute effort to hold myself together just a little longer. It was a gesture I was to repeat often during the following months.

Nevertheless, I managed to dispose of the business; it was a break-even sort of sale. Of my personal possessions, I arranged to store those few things I wanted to save, then sold or gave away the rest; sent change-of-address cards to all and sundry; and, in general, tried to keep myself so busy I wouldn't have time to grieve. David's life insurance paid off all our outstanding debts, including the final four payments on the car. And there was enough left over to open a meager savings account.

Then, in January, the attorney wrote to say probate had closed. With the letter, he sent the key to the front door of the House on Wiffen Cove. The other keys, he informed me, were in the safekeeping of one Stephen Enders, of Enders and Enders, a real estate firm that was caretaking the property until I should arrive.

As anxious as I was to see my new home, it was another three months before I actually set out for Washington State and the House on Wiffen Cove. First, it was the weather. I was not prepared to brave the blizzards, the icy mountain roads, the snow-clogged passes that lie between California and Oregon in the dead of winter.

Then in March, just as the spring thaw began, Emma, who was never sick a day in her life, had a severe heart attack. I couldn't leave until she was out of danger and on her feet once more.

So it wasn't until June 25, almost a year to the day since David's death, that I finally left *our* house. It had been my home since the day David and I returned from our honeymoon nine long years past. Holding myself very stiff, very straight, I put the keys on the kitchen counter for the landlord and, without a backward glance, walked out.

The cats, I took to the Tuttles. They had agreed to care for them as long as necessary. Emma and Jerry, bless them, loved those fat felines almost as much as did I. I knew they would be safe and happy in the Tuttles' home until I was able to take them back once more.

Emma cried when I left. "I know what you've been through, honey," she said, "but I hate to see you go off all alone like this."

"It's what I need, Emma," I assured her. "I'll never be able to put the past behind me . . . get on with my life here. There are too many memories. . . ."

What I didn't say was that for me, the house plus income were like a gift from on high. With a roof over my head and money to live on, I felt certain I could lose myself, my pain and loneliness, in my painting.

Emma blew her nose and tried to smile. Jerry put his arm around her.

"Promise you won't worry," I pleaded.

She nodded.

"Don't spoil those three lazy cats too much." Suddenly I felt the tears welling in my own throat. I threw my arms about Emma and Jerry in turn, giving them each a bear hug; then turned and climbed into the car, backed out of the driveway, and headed north.

Three days later, right on schedule, I crossed the Washington/Oregon border, and still I followed Interstate 5 North. By late afternoon, I reached Olympia, capital of Washington State. From there I took Highway 101 up the Olympic Peninsula through thick forests of dogwood, hemlock, and alder, spruce, cedar, and fir. To my left, as I sped along, I could see the snow-crowned Olympic Mountains, and scarcely a mile without a pond or lake until at last, as the road curved round to the west, to my right I saw at last the white-capped waters of the Strait of Juan de Fuca. It was too dark for sight-seeing by the time I reached historic Port Townsend, so I drove straight on to Port Angeles, where I spent the night.

I had intended to catch the morning ferry, but I overslept. It is only a half-hour trip from Port Angeles, across the Strait of Juan de Fuca, to that small seaward island named Saturday, but there are only two sailings a day: 7 A.M. and 5:30 P.M.

Having missed the early departure, I did not waste time just waiting around. Port Angeles is a charming old town, rich in history and local color. I spent most of the morning browsing; after lunch I drove up to Hurricane Ridge, which provides a spectacular view of the Olympics, Puget Sound with its myriad, emerald-green islands, and the majestic sweep of the Pacific Ocean.

I was back in town, waiting in line for the ferry, by five o'clock.

On board at last, I climbed immediately to the forward deck, eager to catch my first glimpse of Saturday Island. Damp salt wind blowing across the ferryboat's prow swirled about me—stung my eyes, whipped my hair, snatched my breath away. But it was invigorating, too; and leaning against the rail, I watched, enchanted, until the entrance to the harbor came into view.

Though it was now late afternoon, this far north the sun still rode high in the sky, bathing the small port town spread out along the shore and up the steeply sloping hill behind in brilliant light.

The breeze was redolent of kelp, and fish, and briny ocean water. Seagulls wheeled and shrilled above as the ferry nosed into the slip. And now I was aware of people on the dock. Somewhere a dog barked and the unmistakable sound of children's laughter carried over the water.

For the first time since leaving California I felt a twinge of excitement. How different, how appealing, this small town with its quaint Victorian houses nestled amid the lush and endless green of cedar and fir, of roiling vines, bushes, and lacy fern.

Suddenly, a voice boomed forth from the loudspeaker urging all drivers to return to their vehicles. Hurriedly, I made my way to the lower deck and slipped behind the wheel of my car as the ferry was made fast. I drove ashore, following the arrows that pointed the way uphill to the city center, three blocks above the waterfront. There, I turned right onto Main Street, then glanced at my watch. It was after six o'clock.

"Botheration!" I muttered. It was too late now to contact Stephen Enders as I had planned. Well, this far north, the sun wouldn't set until almost nine o'clock. There was still plenty of time to drive out to Wiffen Cove and see the house. But first I needed something to eat.

I stopped at a café called Mom's Place. It was small, shiny clean, and homey. I had a bowl of clam chowder, two cups of coffee, and a piece of homemade apple pie. When I had finished, I asked the young man behind the cash register if he could direct me to Wiffen Cove.

He started, then eyed me with wary curiosity.

Taken aback, I asked, "Is something wrong?"

He shrugged. "It's up the coast a ways . . . about ten miles. Ya can't miss it . . . big place."

I hesitated, wondering if I should again question his initial odd reaction, but decided I'd probably misunderstood. So I thanked him, returned to my car, and drove on. Although the road was paved and well marked, it was also narrow with many twistings and turnings, uphill and down, following the curve of the island's coastline.

The odometer had just moved past the ten-mile mark when I reached the top of a hill, and there below me, surrounded by tall, thick-growing evergreens, was the house. I pulled to the side of the road and parked. I knew it had to be *my* house because it sat atop a promontory above a spit of land that jutted out into the strait, like a finger, cradling in its crook a small rocky cove.

The house itself was a brooding, pseudo-Edwardian monstrosity with gabled second-floor windows and a Victorian pepper-shaker tower. Its air of desolation was heightened by a mass of angry dark clouds blowing in from the sea.

I shivered, put the car in gear, and continued along the road that now curved inland. I lost sight of the house almost immediately; however, the prominence on which it sat dominated the skyline. When I reached the place that I surmised to be directly in back of the house, I found that a sturdy fence stretched between the roadway and the property. A bit farther along, branching off to the right, I discovered a bridge and narrow private road that I could only assume led to the house. However, the way was barred by a heavy wooden gate.

I pulled up to the barrier and got out. To my surprise, I found that it was secured by a single hasp, which I removed without difficulty; then a sturdy shove, and despite its dilapidated appearance, the gate swung back smoothly on well-oiled hinges.

Finding the gate unlocked and unguarded was not reassuring, and I felt a flicker of irritation. In January, when I had postponed my arrival, the attorney had assured me that a fulltime caretaker, to be retained by Enders and Enders, would safeguard the property until such time as I should request the service be terminated. If I found the place vandalized . . .

On the other hand, I thought, had the gate been locked, I could not have gotten in. With a philosophic shrug, I climbed back into my car and started up the driveway. It was all too apparent that if there were someone caretaking the house, that someone was not taking care of the grounds. The roadway was rutted and overgrown with weeds and fern. Still, it was passable, and I pushed on, following its upward curve around the hill.

As I neared the summit, I could feel my heart beating a light, nervous tattoo against my ribs. What would I find when I was at last face to face, so to speak, with my new home? It was a question that was by turns exciting and frightening. What if this place was old and run-down, full of cobwebs and mildew, with a leaky roof and who knew what else?

I had reached the crest of the hill. I held my breath as, for the first time, I beheld at close range my very own home. I braked automatically, all the while staring at the house. It was far larger than I had expected it to be. The back was two stories high, the front rose to three, and a tower, dressed in weathered fish-scale shingles, stood another floor above that. From where I sat, I could see a number of windows, but there was no sign of broken glass. However, some of the gingerbread was a bit worse for wear, and the entire structure needed a new coat of paint.

The road approached the house from an angle, then split into a Y. One arm led around to the back, presumably to the garage; the other passed under a porte cochere, from where it curled round and back upon itself. Slowly, I put the car in gear, drove forward under the portico, then killed the engine.

I sat for a moment, listening to the silence. How peaceful it was. Slowly, I opened the door and got out. Again I paused, stared across the car's roof at the entry: a pair of heavy, ironbound doors. It was quite obvious that the key sent me by the attorney would never open the massive lock securing this entrance.

But the door that fitted my key must be somewhere. Resolutely I walked around my car to the corner of the house. Again I stopped, utterly entranced. This, obviously, was the front of the house. What had once been beds of roses flanked a graceful half-moon veranda. From its base, a wide expanse of ragged lawn sloped downward to the cliff's edge.

From here, the distant murmur of waves lapping the shore was audible, and the view was magnificent, kaleidoscopic. Even as I watched, a shaft of sunlight broke through the shifting clouds to bathe one small offshore island in pale gold radiance while beyond, the sky, the clouds, the waters of the Pacific Ocean, all merged into a soft blue-gray haze. It was hauntingly beautiful. How David would have loved it. . . .

Without warning, a wave of loneliness threatened

to overwhelm me. Quickly, I turned away, continued along the path to the veranda, and hence to the entrance: a high-arched Venetian doorway flanked by elaborate panels of stained glass. My key turned easily in the lock, silently the door opened, and I stepped inside. When I released my hold on the handle, the door swung shut behind me with a gentle swoosh.

Silence, thick as honey, closed in about me. Light, stained blue and yellow and red as it filtered through the panes of colored glass washed over me like waves of murky water, and I realized I was struggling to catch my breath. A faint exotic scent, familiar yet elusive, lingered in the stale, musty air. Abruptly a memory popped into my head: "Aunt Sylvia always smelled good. . . ." I shivered.

As my eyes adjusted to the gloom, my pulse quickened. I don't know what I had expected, but certainly not what I saw. I was standing on an expanse of highly polished black marble. On its far side, two steps led up to a wide landing on which stood a huge bishop's chair, black with age. To my left, a floating stairway of golden oak curved up and around, and when I leaned my head back, I could look straight to the top of the third level. On my right, there was a cloakroom.

On the back wall, framing the bishop's chair, hung two portraits: one was of a dark-haired woman with pale, ivory skin and cold, piercing black eyes; the other was of a man with equally piercing black eyes and a thick, lustrous black beard. Their costumes would have been in fashion in the late 1800s, so the woman could not have been

Sylvia. They both appeared to be staring at me, and suddenly I felt like a trespasser.

But that was ridiculous. After all, the house did belong to me. The attorney had sent me a key, for goodness' sake. Nevertheless, my feet dragged as I crossed the marble slab and mounted the two steps to the landing.

To the right of the bishop's chair was a wide arched opening. Taking a deep breath to steady myself, I stepped through into a fairly large and completely windowless room. However, a pair of sliding doors in the opposite wall stood open and enough light fell through for me to see. What I saw looked like something out of a Victorian guide to interior decoration.

At one end of the room, an elegant little fireplace nestled within a white-painted wooden mantel decorated with harp-strumming cherubs all flashed with gold leaf. At the other end, standing on a low dais, was a small grand piano, also painted white and flashed with gold. A number of delicate straight-backed Louis Quatorze chairs were grouped before it.

The walls, where they extended above an elegant linenfold wainscoting, were covered with faded silk in a large, florid pattern; and high overhead hung an ornate rococo ceiling where white plasterwork cherubs, trailing their gauzy raiment, floated amid a sea of flowers and vines. They, too, were flashed with gold.

Intriguing though it was, I did not linger in the music room, as I came to call it, but moved on through the sliding doors into a long narrow antechamber. This room was completely devoid of furniture. A row of tall leaded windows draped in heavy crimson brocade extended the length of the back wall. At either end marble statues of the Muses stood guard over closed doors.

I chose the door to my left and moved on. As I proceeded with my exploration, moving slowly from room to room, I found it increasingly difficult to credit my senses. The lower floor was a warren of small chambers tied loosely together by dark, narrow halls of varying length.

And as I moved deeper into the house, I caught myself stopping to listen to the silence, glancing over my shoulder, walking on tiptoe over those floors that were uncarpeted lest the click of my heels betray my presence. I kept telling myself I was being ridiculous. So I was being ridiculous—the unwelcome sensation did not go away. There was something *creepy* about the silence—the shadows.

A peculiar musty odor pervaded many of these rooms, and all were furnished without discernible rhyme or reason. Every wall was closely hung with paintings and photographs; every available surface was crowded with a hodgepodge of figurines, ornate filigree boxes, porcelain jars and vases—there was even a feather fan and an ivory opium pipe. One room was dedicated to a vast collection of seashells. It was mind-boggling!

And all the while, as I moved deeper into the old house, I was aware of a prickly sensation up the back of my neck, of goosebumps down my arms, as if unfriendly eyes were fixed upon me. But I refused to let my childish fears deter me. I was determined to see it all. It was my house!

The furniture included everything from small Victorian marble-topped tables and bowls filled with silk roses, to an early American horsehair sofa. And there were cabinets filled with dishes and silver and linens, and bookcases lined with books, all squeezed into whatever space was available, and for the most part, everything was covered by a fine haze of dust.

Many of the pieces were quite beautiful and, I thought, possibly valuable. It was rather like wandering through a museum and I should have enjoyed myself immensely had it not been for that unsettling sensation of being watched.

Oddly enough, several rooms were dust-free. They were also free of that peculiar musty smell, but even those rooms had an untidy look: here a half-drawn blind, a cup and saucer on a lamp table, a drawer standing ajar. In one room, there was a pair of slippers—elegant satin mules, actually—left under a chair. It was almost as if someone had been there only moments before, and every time I opened a door, I half-expected to find Aunt Sylvia waiting to greet me.

It was—disturbing. Had someone been staying there? A caretaker, perhaps? If so, where was that person now? Were those mules Aunt Sylvia's, or was the caretaker a woman?

It was a relief when I opened a door and found myself in a large, relatively airy place, a formal dining room. Its back wall was hung with shimmering oriental tapestries; while the walls at either end were paneled from floor to ceiling in golden oak and inset with elegant fireplaces sporting magnificent brass firedogs. A long rectangular table, fourteen chairs, and a huge sideboard were all finished in Chinese black lacquer inlaid with mother-of-pearl.

Other than the music room, this was the only spacious and elegantly furnished room on the ground floor.

By the time I had completed my inspection of the ground floor, it was growing late and the light in the house was beginning to dim. In the hall off the kitchen, I found the back stairs and paused for a moment considering a visit to the upper regions; but I decided I had seen enough for one day.

To be honest, that sense of unease that had followed me all through the house had grown stronger in direct relation to the dimming of the light. Although I tried to brush the thought aside, the impression that I was not alone was now almost overpowering.

With a final nervous glance about, I made my way back to the entry as quickly as I could, stepped outside, and locked the door behind me with a pronounced sense of relief. Then I turned, walked to the edge of the veranda, and surveyed what had at one time been a lovely formal garden. From the foot of the veranda steps, a flagstone path, barely visible through the long ragged grass, led by a circuitous route around a forlorn and tipsy little birdbath, through flower beds overgrown and gone to seed, to the cliff's edge.

The depressing clouds that had marred my arrival at Wiffen Cove had blown away while I was inside, and now the sun, though nearing the horizon, shone bright once more. Birds were calling in the trees, the earthy scent of growing things filled the air. My spirits began to rise, the path beckoned. Smiling, I skipped down the steps and followed the flagstones to the cliff's edge. There, I found myself looking down a long flight of wooden steps to the cove far below.

I gazed down at that quiet beach where the water, stained gold by the westering sun, lapped gently at a narrow strip of gleaming sand. I listened to the soft sighing of the breeze, felt its touch, like gentle fingers in my hair, like cool lips upon my brow. . . .

*Oh, David* . . . The joy I had felt only moments before turned to grief inside me, and I sank down on the top step, buried my face in my hands.

I could not name the emotions churning inside me: loneliness, rapture, guilt, foreboding. Neither do I know how long I sat there. But when at last I raised my head, the sun had sunk beneath the horizon and the dusk of evening was deepening perceptibly with each passing moment. A sudden chill wind raised goosebumps down my bare arms. I rose to my feet and turned back toward the spot where I had parked my car.

Beneath the dense stand of trees bordering the lawn, the blackness was complete and I stared warily over my shoulder as I moved across the unkempt grass, stumbling on the uneven ground. As a child, I was terrified of the night. Now I wasn't exactly frightened, but since then I have always been uneasy in the dark.

I had just reached the porte cochere when out of the blackness a wild, high-pitched, inhuman ululation seemed to erupt all around me. Gone as quickly as it had come, that savage cry halted me in my tracks, then sent me sprinting for the safety of my car. Every nerve in my body screamed *hurry, hurry, hurry!* and I broke a fingernail in my haste to open the door and jump in.

Once behind the wheel, I forced myself to breathe deeply, assuring myself the sound was only some animal or a trick of the wind. Just lean back, relax, I told myself. You're safe here in the car. There is nothing to fear. As I continued my mantra, my muscles relaxed. Slowly, I leaned back, then froze. Something had brushed the back of my head.

For one agonized moment I was paralyzed by sheer terror while through my mind rushed the thought, *You fool! You didn't lock the car when you got out!* An instant longer I sat, my breath aching in my throat, while every horror story I have ever heard about lone women in lonely places flashed through my mind. Then, determined to defend myself as best I could, I grabbed up the flashlight that lay on the seat beside me and spun about.

There was nothing there—only my sweater, dangling from the hook above the window frame, one sleeve hanging down behind me. Still trembling, I forced myself to lean over and look behind the seat for whatever might be hiding there. Absolutely nothing.

I settled back and took several deep breaths, willing the hysteria to subside. Only then did I suddenly remember I still hadn't locked the doors! In one sweeping motion I remedied that situation. Then I started the car, drove forward, out from under the porte cochere, and followed the roadway off the property. When I crossed over the bridge, I neglected to stop to close the heavy gate behind me. Perhaps I should have, but it was truly night by then and I would not, under any circumstances, have gotten out of the car.

Back on the highway, driving toward the small

town once more, I chided myself for letting my imagination run away with me. Slowly, my pulse rate returned to normal. In any event, I told myself, it had been a bit of an adventure.

A few moments later, I was exceedingly glad to see the lights of the town twinkling through the darkness. I checked into the Sea Urchin Motel, went across the street to Mom's Place for a hamburger, and was in bed by ten. But sleep did not come readily. I kept thinking about the House on Wiffen Cove, the grounds, that weird sound and the one thing that kept worrying me, something I couldn't quite put my finger on. . . .

At last my mind began to drift, floating twixt wakefulness and sleep, in that state when thought and dream begin to blend. And then it hit me, sent an icy chill washing over me. My sweater. At Wiffen Cove, when I got out of the car to go into the house, I had left that sweater lying across my bag in the backseat. I never, ever, hang anything on that hook above the car window.

# TWO

I was walking in a wood. In the distance I could hear voices. And music. I walked faster, almost floating over the ground and it occurred to me that if I wanted to, I could fly; but when I looked upward, I saw that the trees' branches twined thickly overhead, like a tightly woven net.

And even as I stared, somehow, I was sitting on a huge flat stone high on the edge of a cliff. On the beach below me, a group of figures shrouded in long black cloaks sat about a camp fire laughing and singing, and from time to time, one of them would jump up, throw off his cloak, and frolic, yet fully clothed, into the waves that washed ever higher along the shore.

I watched them, and I was filled with loneliness and dread. Then, I don't know how, someone was beside me, and I knew it was David. He put his arms around me and pressed his face against my breast. I ran my fingers over his bare shoulders, down his back, savoring the feel of him, pressing my own body against the lovely silken warmth of his. My heart was beating hard and fast, each nerve aflame and throbbing with desire.

His hands, so gentle, so knowing, began to move

slowly down my back while his fingers explored each curve of my body, caressing, teasing; and the tip of his tongue traced tiny whorls of excitement over my eager breasts, kindling an exquisite and unbearable need. I closed my eyes, my body moving now of its own volition; but that final moment of ecstasy eluded me and suddenly I realized that the rock upon which we lay had begun to tremble, to turn and pitch and toss.

I saw that what I had thought was a huge boulder was really a boat, and all around us the black water stretched, boiling and heaving as if in the throes of a mighty storm, and slowly the deck beneath us began to tip, ever more steeply. Then David seemed to melt from within my clinging arms and, filled with horror, I watched as he rolled down, down, toward that ghastly black water. I tried to cry out, tried to catch him fast.

For one awful moment he teetered on the edge of the deck, his arms reaching out to me, his eyes begging for help, but I could not move. Then he was gone, and the pain and terror that flooded through me remained, even after it woke me, and I lay shivering, tears falling from my eyes.

# THREE

I was still lying, wide-eyed, when morning came. I watched the first gray light of dawn brighten to rose, and yet I did not move. I willed myself to think of nothing, to remember nothing. . . .

Only when my mind was empty and calm did I rise and dress, and when I stepped outside, I greeted the fresh new morning with a smile. The offshore breeze carried with it the salty tang of the sea, and I drew in several deep bracing breaths as I crossed the road to Mom's Place.

While I ate an English muffin dripping with butter, cream cheese, and homemade strawberry jam, I thought about that sweater hanging on the hook above the window in my car. Either I had hung it there—possible but highly unlikely—or some stranger had been in my car. So, I told myself, even if it were some stranger, what then? Nosy but hardly sinister. But why pick up my sweater and hang it on that hook over the window? Cheeky, but still, hardly sinister. Somehow, sitting there listening to the homey clatter of dishes, the calm murmur of voices punctuated by quiet laughter, the whole episode suddenly seemed less threatening.

Nevertheless, I promised myself that in future I'd

avoid getting caught alone in such a deserted location after dark. At the thought, a wry smile twisted my lips. Owning a home so far removed from others, I'd be spending a lot of time alone in a *deserted* spot! But, I promised myself, I'll be inside with the doors bolted. And, in any event, it would be a long time before I'd forget to lock my car—even when I left it in the driveway!

As for that weird sound that had so terrified me, who knew what strange animals prowled the woods up here in the great Pacific Northwest? Suddenly, I grinned, remembering stories I had read about some fantastic creature called Big Foot that supposedly inhabited the forests in this part of the world. Well, I could be certain it wasn't Big Foot—everyone agreed he had a stench that would make a skunk envious. With that thought, I dismissed the whole business from my mind.

I drank one more cup of coffee, paid the check, and set out in search of Enders and Enders. The office, which I located without difficulty, was in a small remodeled house not too far from the ferry landing. Inside, I was greeted by a pleasant, gray-haired woman who informed me that Mr. Enders was out of the office for the morning. "He'll be back about three," she said. "Could I give him a message?"

"Perhaps you could help me?"

"Perhaps," she agreed.

"The House on Wiffen Cove . . ."

The woman continued to smile but the expression in her eyes underwent a subtle change even as I spoke. She shook her head. "No . . . I'm sorry, but no. The house is not for sale." She rose to her feet and with the expertise of long practice, ushered me across the office and out onto the sidewalk again before I could open my mouth to protest.

I stood there for a moment staring at the office door. Finally I shrugged and turned away. I guess it's true, I thought. People in small towns do have their own peculiar ways. I glanced at my watch. It was only half past ten. The woman had said Mr. Enders would be back at three. And so will I, I promised myself.

I decided to spend the meantime looking about the town. First I took a quick walking tour of the business district, which was a maze of boutiques, souvenir shops, and fast food stands all clustered about the harbor. Then I returned to my car and drove up the hill to the main street, which ran parallel to the waterfront. Dotted along its length were the post office, an ancient library, and a small courthouse.

At its north end, where Mom's Place and the Sea Urchin Motel were located, it merged into the county road that led past Wiffen Cove. Having already been along that route, I turned to the south and followed the thoroughfare as it wound around the business district and down to parallel the shoreline.

I drove slowly, taking time to look about me as I went. To the west, on the hill above the road, surrounded by carefully manicured lawns, were a number of lovely old Victorian houses, several with TO LET signs tucked discreetly into the corner of a bay window.

On the opposite side, there was a narrow parkway atop a low rocky bluff. Juniper and pine, like brood-

ing sentinels, stood watch along its brow and, inter-
spersed among the trees, were several old and
weathered benches fashioned from the trunk of
some fallen giant. Offshore, thrusting up through
the rippling water, a huge bleak boulder jutted sky-
ward like some titan's spear magically frozen in
time and space.

I pulled my car to the curb and got out. There was
not a soul visible in either direction, the only sound
the whispering of branches swayed by a passing
breeze. The sunlight was warm on my head and
shoulders, but the breeze off the water was cool.

I crossed the road and stepped up into the parkway. The grass was thick and soft underfoot and I
strolled along, drinking in the freshness of the air,
admiring the flowers that bloomed in the gardens
across the street. Then, wooed by the soft susurration of water over sand, I left the path, moved closer
to the cliff's edge.

The land fell away sheer, a drop of perhaps ten
feet, to a narrow rocky strip of land where wavelets
broke, ebbed, and flowed amid a welter of flotsam
and jetsam. It was just the sort of beach along which
I like to stroll, poking into the shallow tide pools,
picking and choosing among the welter of treasure
cast up by the changeling tides. I glanced right and
left, searching for a way down, but there was none,
which set me to wondering that no sort of guardrail
had been erected along that precipitous edge.

I took a hasty step back as it occurred to me how
dangerous a place it was, even on a clear calm day
like today. It was not hard to imagine how on a wild
and stormy night the wind would whip the water
into angry waves, fling them against that wall of

stone with a mighty roar, sending icy froth and spray flying. Woe, then, to anyone who drew too near the edge and lost his footing.

Suddenly depressed by my gloomy thoughts, I glanced about. Still nary a soul in sight, and not too far ahead, the path disappeared into a thick stand of evergreens. Time, I decided, to go back to my car. But as I turned, a glimmer of sunlight on a pane of glass deep in the grove of trees caught my eye.

My curiosity piqued, I continued forward, into the shadows under the pines, until I came upon a weathered wooden sign suspended between two equally weathered posts: MADELINNE HOUSE. And beneath the name, in small letters: Lunch—11:30 to 3:00; Dinner—5:00 to midnight. Just beyond, at the water's edge, stood what must at one time have been the most elegant house in town. However, with the passing of the years, it had obviously been converted into a very posh resort.

I glanced at my watch. One o'clock. Just time for lunch before I should return to the offices of Enders and Enders.

While I waited to be seated, I noted that the dining room was not large; but an illusion of unlimited space was created by a wall of tinted glass that invited the eye to gaze outward across slowly undulating waters that stretched, unobstructed, to a hazy horizon.

The hostess showed me to a table beside the glass wall, a vantage point from which I could get a clear view of the rocky bluff along which I had just come. I gave the waitress my order, then turned my attention outward once more.

From where I was sitting, I now had an excellent

view of the narrow strip of rough, steeply slanted beach at the foot of the cliff. The exposed rocks were green with sea moss. Long strings of kelp twined round their bases and coiled amid the jumble of derelict logs that floated in and out as the waters of the strait rose and fell. If only there were steps down . . .

The waitress returned with my salad and I glanced up just as a tall, attractive man entered the dining room. He stopped, stood staring at the floor, obviously lost in thought. When he abruptly raised his head, our eyes met. A startled expression flashed across his face to be replaced immediately by a smile. He turned and nodded to the hostess, then crossed directly to my table.

"Hello," he said, "I'm Stephen Enders, and you are the woman who was inquiring about the house on Wiffen Cove."

"Yes I am. How did you know?"

"May I?" he asked, pulling out the chair opposite mine and sitting down. Then he added, "I called the office and Vera told me you had been in . . . her description was accurate. I'd have recognized you even if the dining room had been crowded."

The implied compliment didn't fool me a bit. How hard can it be to recognize a woman with bright red hair? Then I noticed the way he was staring at me, as if I were a chocolate éclair and he a chocoholic. I froze. As long as I was married to David, how other men viewed me had been without threat or promise. But now I was a widow and totally unprepared to cope with the feeling of vulnerability the frank admiration in this man's eyes awoke in me. I think I blushed.

However, the approach of the waitress drew Ender's attention away, giving me time to regain my composure; and while he was busy ordering his lunch, I was able to study him unobserved. His hair, graying at the temples, grew thick and curly above a wide forehead. Dark brows arched above gray eyes. His nose and chin were strong, the mouth firm. His suit, well cut and perfectly tailored, was worn over a turtleneck sweater—I'd have bet money it was cashmere. On his right hand he wore a massive onyx and gold ring set with one large diamond. Real estate business on this small island must be very lucrative.

While Enders and the waitress were still discussing the merits of the luncheon steak versus the catch-of-the-day, my gaze wandered back to the rocky shoreline below us. And even as I watched, the waters began to lick the base of the cliff. The tide had risen several inches in the short span of time since Stephen Enders entered the dining room. I remembered how only a short while before I had contemplated a stroll along that beach. A chill ran through me as my imagination conjured up a picture of some hapless woman clawing at that sheer rocky bank while the rising water swirled about her ankles, her knees. . . .

I jumped at the sound of Enders's voice.

"Sorry. Didn't mean to startle you." The waitress was gone and he was smiling at me.

I shook my head. "My fault. I was wool-gathering. . . ." I picked up my water tumbler and took a sip.

"I'm afraid Vera didn't get your name."

I was tempted to say that *Vera* hadn't given me a

chance to give my name, but I didn't. Instead I said, "I'm Kimberly D'Ahl."

The waitress brought our coffee. Enders picked up his cup, took a swallow, regarding me thoughtfully all the while. Finally he said, "So you're Sylvia's heir." He sighed, took another swallow of coffee. "Do you intend to live in the house?"

"I most certainly do."

"Perhaps you should take a look at the property before you decide."

"Actually," I admitted, "I drove up there yesterday and looked around. . . ."

The smile faded from his lips and his look sharpened. "How did you get in? The gate . . ."

Again I blushed, feeling unaccountably guilty. "The gate wasn't locked. I just pushed it open and drove up there. Mr. Howell, my attorney, sent me a house key."

Enders made no further comment, just stared at me thoughtfully. The waitress returned, refilled our coffee cups.

"I went in . . . walked all through the place . . . at least the ground floor. I must say I found it a bit overpowering."

A smile flickered across Enders's face. "It does tend to have that effect on the uninitiated."

"Incidentally, does anyone live out there now . . . or near there?" Although I could see no point in mentioning the incident with my sweater, I couldn't help thinking a plausible explanation would be comforting. As for the slippers and the cup and saucer, I felt certain they were just as Sylvia had left them since I had not asked to have the place cleaned before my arrival.

Enders's eyes were searching my face. "Why do you ask?"

"No reason . . . I just wondered."

"Old houses can give one strange feelings," Enders commented dryly.

"I suppose so," I agreed.

"You might find a newer place more comfortable . . . something closer to town. . . ."

"Perhaps . . . nonetheless, I intend to take possession of the House on Wiffen Cove immediately."

Enders offered no further comment and I continued, "Since your firm has had the responsibility for caretaking, I wanted to check with you first. . . ."

I waited for him to offer some information—anything—but he didn't speak and the silence lengthened.

At last I asked, "What happened to the caretaker?"

"Caretaker?"

"Mr. Howell wrote me that Aunt Sylvia had someone who looked after the grounds. He said you would keep him on as caretaker until I arrived."

Enders shook his head. "Must have been a misunderstanding. Sylvia never had a regular groundskeeper living at Wiffen Cove, and I didn't think one necessary . . . just an added expense. We don't have any trouble with vandals here on the island . . . the sheriff drives by regularly and checks on things."

Again the silence fell. Enders devoted himself to the blackened halibut he had ordered. I sipped my coffee.

Finally, he looked up. "I'd have gotten someone

out there to mow the lawn and get things ready if I'd known when you were arriving."

Funny, I thought. I had expected the attorney to notify Enders of my anticipated arrival. Aloud, I said, "It's all right. I didn't know what to expect so I wasn't disappointed."

"I'll take care of it right away, if you like."

"I'd appreciate it," I said. "But the main reason why I wanted to see you is that I'd like to know a little more about the house. How old is it? Do you think the wiring and plumbing are safe? Can you recommend someone to give me an estimate on any repair work that needs to be done? Do you know someone who could be trusted to look at the contents of that house and tell me what's valuable and what isn't?" I was ticking items off on my fingers as quickly as I could think of them.

"Wait a minute . . . slow down!" Laughing, Enders raised a defensive hand. "One thing at a time, please!"

I laughed, too. "Sorry . . . guess I got carried away."

We had finished our lunch by that time and Enders suggested we drive out to Wiffen Cove. "We can look the place over and discuss your concerns at the same time."

As we left the restaurant he said, "Let's take my car," and he guided me across the parking lot to a low-slung silver-gray Porsche. He started to open the door, then looked down at me. "Will you make the necessary decisions, or will Mr. D'Ahl be joining us?"

Once more I wondered if Mr. Howell had not told Enders anything about me. I don't know why I didn't tell him the truth immediately, that David was dead, that I had been a widow for a year. But I didn't. I simply said, "I'll make all the decisions."

"I see," he muttered. I wondered if he really did.

Once he was settled behind the wheel, he asked, "Do you mind if we run by the office first? There are a couple of things I must attend to. It won't take a minute."

"No problem," I assured him.

As he pulled the car to a stop in front of the office, he said, "If you'd like to wait here, I'll be right back."

Enders left the office door open behind him when he entered. As I lost sight of his retreating back, my gaze encountered Vera. She stood behind her desk, ramrod straight, glaring at someone who remained out of my range of vision. Enders, I assumed. She was speaking vehemently, shaking her head angrily from side to side. Suddenly she clamped her lips tight and leaned forward, hands pressed palm down upon her desktop, glaring. Thus she remained for a long moment; then, slowly, she sank back into her chair. From the expression on her face, it was clear that she had lost the argument.

Moments later, Stephen Enders returned to the car. He wasn't smiling, exactly, but it was obvious that he was pleased with himself. For some reason, I found that irritating. I turned my head and gazed out the window while he started the engine, pulled out into the road. Within minutes, we had left the town behind us.

I turned back to him then, and asked, "Can you tell me something about the house . . . its history?"

Enders took a deep breath, let it out slowly. "Well, it was built sometime in the 1860s by an old gold miner who had struck it rich and wanted to settle down." Enders paused while he negotiated a sharp turn. "They say he drew up the house plans himself."

"He should have hired an architect," I muttered under my breath.

Enders appeared not to have heard. "He was a bachelor . . . his sister came out here from New York to run his household for him and act as his hostess. The old man had great plans . . . great plans. . . ."

There was an odd tone in Enders's voice and I glanced at him inquiringly. Just then we reached the turnoff and he pulled the car to a stop. The gate that I had left wide open when I made my retreat the night before was inexplicably closed, and I could see that a length of rusty chain held together by an equally rusty padlock now fastened it securely to the gatepost.

Enders gave me an odd look. "Did you provide the lock?"

I shook my head. "No, I left the gate open. . . ."

Frowning, he reached into the glove compartment. "I've got some skeleton keys here. Perhaps one of them will fit."

He got out, and after a few tries, the lock snapped open. He was scowling when he climbed back into the car. "Sheriff probably saw it standing open and decided to take care of it," he muttered, talking more to himself than to me.

He put the car in gear and we drove in silence up the rutted, overgrown road. He pulled to a stop on the spot where I had parked the previous day, and killed the engine. For a moment he gazed moodily out the window, then commented, "The old man really never got to enjoy it. . . ."

"The old man? Oh. The one who built the place. So why didn't he get to enjoy it?"

"He died shortly after he moved in."

"How sad," I murmured. "This great big house . . ." After a moment of contemplation, I asked, "Who did live in it?"

"The miner's sister . . . his only heir." Enders sighed, then opened the car door. "Come," he said. "Let's get out and have a look."

As we walked toward the entrance, I asked, "How long did Sylvia Belgedes live here?"

At that moment we turned the corner of the house. Without a word, we both stopped, stood gazing down across the expanse of unkempt lawn to the vista of water and islands and blue sky beyond. It seemed even more beautiful than I remembered.

So lost was I in contemplation of that view, I only half-listened while Enders explained, "It was sold in the late sixties for back taxes . . . to a man named LeBeauforte. He and Sylvia lived here until he died . . . about ten years ago. He left everything to her. Sylvia became sort of a recluse after that. . . ."

"Did you know her?" I asked.

"Know her? Yes . . . I knew Sylvia. I liked to think we were friends."

I looked at him in surprise. "Don't you know if you were her friend?"

He smiled at me. "I tried to be a good friend to Sylvia, but she was . . . difficult to know." He paused, then added, "But why all the questions . . . didn't you know her?"

I shook my head. We had started walking again, and when we reached the entry, I gave Enders my key. He opened the door and we stepped inside.

"Do you want to see the lower floor again?"

"No. I'd like to see the upstairs today, please."

Our inspection of the second floor did not take long. It contained six large bedrooms and four remarkably modern bathrooms.

"LeBeauforte," Enders explained, "had the baths put in, and Sylvia had them and the kitchen modernized and all the plumbing and wiring brought up to code about 1983."

The master bedroom was lovely. I would have liked to spend more time there, exploring the closets, admiring the huge four-poster, the oriel window—the view from the alcove was panoramic and altogether lovely.

*How David would love this place.* The thought caught me unawares, and suddenly, childishly, I didn't want Enders there. I turned on my heel and left the room quickly. "Come on," I said. "Let's see the third floor while we're here."

As we started up the stairs, Enders asked, "What do you think you are going to find on the third floor?"

It seemed an odd question. I paused and turned to look at him, but his face was perfectly blank. "Why . . . I've no idea," I admitted.

We continued to the landing. On the far side, a circular iron stair continued upward to the cupola; to our left, a pair of wide double doors stood open, giving access to a magnificent ballroom. Slowly, I crossed the intervening space and stopped just inside. The walls, on three sides, were broken at regular six-foot intervals by French doors that opened onto a narrow balcony; and on either side of each doorway, potted palms grew in huge marble urns.

I gave Enders a questioning look. "Don't tell me those trees have survived all this time without watering?"

He grinned. "No. I've had them cared for. It just seemed like the least I could do . . . keep them alive. They were Sylvia's pride and joy."

I nodded, turned my attention back to the room. Between the palms, love seats upholstered in satin damask in shades of palest pink and blue and yellow stood upon short curved legs of polished pecan. Overhead, crystal chandeliers shattered the sun's rays into myriad brilliant rainbows and scattered them over the walls and ceiling.

"It's really quite remarkable, isn't it?" There was pride in Enders's voice.

Must be the salesman in him, I thought. "Like nothing I've ever seen," I agreed.

We stood for a few moments longer, then Enders said, "Those chandeliers . . . all Waterford crystal . . . they're worth a king's ransom."

I nodded, speechless.

Enders continued, "This ballroom was added in 1942 by its then current owner. It was never used."

"Never used!"

He shrugged, stood staring moodily up at the nearest chandelier.

I let my gaze wander again up and down the length of that fantastic room. "You mean, never . . . really never?"

Enders laughed, the sound without humor. "That's what I hear."

"But why build it, then never use it?"

"Maybe it had something to do with the war. . . ."

"How sad," I said. "What a terrible waste. . . ."

We moved back, out of the ballroom. On the landing, we again paused and I asked, "What about downstairs . . . is there anything of value there?"

"I don't really know . . . some of the larger pieces were part of the original furnishings . . . but toward the end, the Crofts did sell a lot of things. . . ."

"Who were the Crofts?"

Enders looked blank, then laughed. "Last family to live in the house before LeBeauforte bought it."

"So most of this stuff was Sylvia's?"

Enders nodded. "Sylvia and Antoine were avid collectors and they never seemed concerned about money."

"Did you know Antoine, too?"

"Not well . . . he traveled a great deal."

We turned, then, to the circular iron stairway. I glanced at my watch and noted that it was already after four.

"I think I'll forego the cupola," I decided. "I really do want to get back before the post office closes." I had told Emma she could write me there care of general delivery.

As we descended the staircase, Enders asked, "When do you plan to move in?"

"To be realistic . . . the sooner the better." I stared sidewise at him, wondering just how frank I should be. My limited finances were dwindling fast, but the trust account now held a rather sizable amount. Should I ask Enders's help and advice?

Before I could make up my mind, he spoke. "You could move in tomorrow. You could have moved in today if I'd known you were coming."

"Well," I said, deciding to tell him the truth, "I can't afford to stay on in town indefinitely, but I just can't move into this house until all that . . . that clutter has been appraised and stored. And the place needs a thorough cleaning."

We had reached the foot of the stairs and he stopped, one hand resting on the newel post. "Getting an appraisal won't be any problem, and I know several people who would be glad to help with the cleaning. The packing and storing would depend on appraised value, of course." His manner was straightforward, businesslike.

"Good," I said. "The sooner it gets done, the better." We continued across the foyer to the door and walked out onto the veranda. Enders locked the door behind us and handed me my key.

A dismal gray overcast obscured the sun, and the breeze over the water was chill. On the drive back to town we reviewed all the things I wanted done, and I made a mental note to contact Mr. Howell as soon as possible about the money in the trust fund. Perhaps some of the money could be used to renovate the house before I moved in.

When Enders dropped me by my car he said, "I'll get started on the things we discussed . . . shouldn't take long."

"Thanks . . . and thanks for taking me through the house."

At the post office, there was only one piece of mail

waiting for me. I walked back to my car and got in before tearing the envelope open. Inside I found a sheet of cheap, lined paper. I unfolded it, then gazed in consternation at the message. Printed in big block letters with bright crimson crayon, it read: WANT TO JOIN SYLVIA? JUST HURRY ON DOWN TO WIFFEN COVE!

# FOUR

I read the note through twice. Slowly the initial shock gave way to anger. Who would want to play such a malicious joke on me—and to what purpose? I looked again at the piece of cheap ruled paper as if I expected a signature to magically appear. Then I searched my memory, trying to think who, besides the attorney, knew I was coming to Saturday Island. Certainly neither Vera nor Stephen had seemed to expect me, but of course they could have been pretending. . . .

I dropped the note on the seat beside me and started the car, intending to go straight to the police. But before putting the engine into gear, I picked up the envelope and looked at it once more. The plain white legal-size envelope had been mailed to my California address. The post office had forwarded it to me here. There was no return address, but the postmark, although blurred, proved that it had been mailed, originally, from the State of Washington. The name of the city and the date were totally illegible.

So I really didn't have anything meaningful to show the police. With a sinking sensation in the pit of my stomach, I realized a trip to the police station would be, in the long run, a waste of their time and mine.

Feeling lonely and depressed, I backed out into the street and returned to the Sea Urchin Motel. Then across the street to Mom's Place for another hamburger, and for the second time, was again in bed by ten o'clock. But I found no comfort in sleep. All that endless night, dreaming, I ran, stumbling, through the shadow-filled rooms and halls of the House on Wiffen Cove, relentlessly pursued by a lank and loathsome figure shrouded in black.

It was the ringing of my bedside phone that finally rescued me—its shrill insistent clamor a lifeline to consciousness. But even after I opened my eyes, my brain, held thrall by the horrors of the slowly fading nightmare, had difficulty recalling where I was or why. When I did pick up the phone, a warm, motherly voice caroled a cheery "good morning" in my ear.

"Ahhhrgh." I almost strangled myself trying to stifle a yawn.

"Oh dear! Did I wake you?"

"Wahoorrrg!" Another monstrous yawn overpowered me.

"I'm so sorry."

"Who is this?" Somewhat less than politely.

"Oh dear. I'm not doing this very gracefully, am I? This is Vera. Perhaps I should ring back later."

The woman from the real estate office! Why in the world would she be calling me? "No . . . it's all right. I should be up."

"I'm so sorry. I just didn't stop to think . . . this is your vacation. Naturally you'd be sleeping late."

What makes her think I'm on vacation? I wondered. "Please, don't apologize," I muttered. "It would be a shame to waste my *vacation* sleeping."

Her little laugh was deferential. "How true . . . but the reason for my call, if you plan to stay in town for a while, I thought we might have lunch. Shall I pick you up about one?"

Her invitation took me totally by surprise. Still sleep muddled and not in the mood for making small talk with a stranger, I opened my mouth to decline. Then the thought hit me, best not to seem unfriendly. After all, I was planning to make this small community my home. Finally, halfheartedly, I agreed. "That would be very nice . . . thank you."

"Good. I'm so glad. It will give us a chance to really get acquainted. See you at one, my dear." I heard the click of the phone as she rang off.

Feeling out-of-sorts and put-upon, I dropped the receiver into its cradle and glanced at my watch. Nine o'clock. My head throbbed and my eyes were itchy. Old busybody, I thought. Then I reminded myself that it wasn't her fault I had had a bad night. She was only trying to make me feel welcome. Sighing, I picked up the phone again and rang the motel office. "Is it possible to have coffee and a newspaper brought to my room?" I asked.

"Don't have room service," came the sullen reply.

"I know that!" I snapped. "I just hoped someone might be willing to run over to Mom's Place for me. There's a good tip in it. . . ." I tempted.

After a grudging silence, the voice said, "Well, whadda ya want . . . might be able to find someone."

"A carafe of coffee with cream, and a newspaper, please."

Twenty minutes later there was a rap on my door and a cheery voice announced, "Got your coffee and paper, miss."

I opened the door and took the tray from a chubby, bright-eyed young woman of perhaps eighteen. Just the smell of the coffee seemed to ease my head and raise my spirits. I set the tray on my bedside table and returned to the door with the promised tip.

The girl glanced quickly at the crumpled bills I laid in her hand, then smiled. "If you need anything else, miss, just ask Mr. Gillings to tell me."

"Thank you, I'd appreciate that." As she turned to go, I called after her, "What's your name?"

"Helen, miss . . . Helen Riley."

I stood in the doorway a moment longer, watching her retreating figure, then turned back into the room and closed the door. After pouring myself some coffee, I crawled back into bed and picked up the paper.

Only then did I note that it was the weekend edition. And that reminded me that today was Sunday. How very strange, I thought, that Vera should want to take me to lunch on Sunday . . . probably her only day off. Unless, of course, she was not the secretary as I had assumed but was a salesperson or a broker. Damn! I thought. Why didn't I think to ask her name?

For all I knew, she might even be the owner. Still, she had seemed less than eager to talk to me the day before. Why this sudden burst of friendliness? Or was it friendliness? Could Vera be the author of that miserable note? I was still toying with that idea two hours later when I got out of bed. It followed me into the shower, nagged at me while I dressed, waited with me until Vera arrived.

Promptly at one, she pulled an old but beautifully cared for Mercedes into the parking space next to my compact. I hurried out, opened the car door, and settled in beside her. After we had exchanged greetings, I said, "It was very thoughtful of you to ask me to lunch."

"Nonsense, my dear. We get so few newcomers here, and I thoroughly enjoy showing off our island."

She started the engine, put the car in gear. "We have only two nice places to eat. Saturday is so small . . . we don't get the visitors that San Juan and Orcas do."

"Then you're not dependent on the tourist trade?"

"Not really, although Madelinne House compares very favorably with Rosario's . . . that's the big resort on Orcas. For the rest, we're mostly retirees with a few summer people, a few artists and craftspeople."

As we talked, Vera guided the car through the city center, then turned east a block above the waterfront. She parked in front of what once had been a small but elegant Victorian home. The steps leading to the front door were guarded by a pair of fearsome, miniature stone lions, and the latticework shading the porch supported an ancient climbing rose, heavy with fragrant pink blossoms.

The hostess greeted Vera warmly; obviously they were old friends. Then she led us upstairs and seated us at a table in a big bay window. There were no menus. Our hostess simply asked if I liked seafood, and when I said yes, she and Vera smiled happily at one another nodding and uttering agreeable ums and ahs.

That settled, Vera and I turned our attention to the view. It was a repeat of the one from Madelinne House, but from our present elevation, the rock that had seemed cold and bleak when I sat looking upward from its base was softened by a crown of scrub evergreen. Above and beyond it, accentuating the cerulean blue of the sky, a flock of little puffy clouds drifted, while stretching outward from its base, the waters of the strait lay still and black beneath a surface ripple of luminous aquamarine. I gazed in awe, my heart suddenly bursting with a kind of wonder I had not felt since the days when David could walk.

When David could walk. . . . Without warning a cold knot formed in the pit of my stomach and I shut my eyes against the stab of pain, the wrench of guilt, remembering brought. But, and I clung desperately to the thought, it wasn't my fault . . . it wasn't. . . .

"Are you all right, my dear?" Vera's voice came to me as from a distance.

For a moment I remained stock still, trying to clear my mind of the unwelcome memories. Only when I was sure I could speak calmly, did I say, "Yes, of course. I was just overcome by this magnificent view."

Pride lighted Vera's face. "It is lovely. I'm so glad you're enjoying it." Even as she spoke, a waitress appeared and set a steaming tureen in the center of our table, and Vera added, "Now, just wait till you taste the lobster bisque."

The food, which included alder-smoked salmon, shrimp-stuffed crab, and deep-fried gooey duck, was perfection! And as we ate, Vera talked easily—mostly about the history of the town. Yet the feeling of unease that had touched me when she first called that morning continued to dig at me. Why, I kept wondering, is she lavishing all this attention, this expense on me?

It wasn't until the table had been cleared, and we were sitting back, enjoying the view, that Vera said, "So you're really serious about the House on Wiffen Cove . . . ?"

My pulse quickened. Now we're going to get to the real reason for this invitation, I thought, but I answered smoothly, "Yes, indeed."

"It is a lovely old place." Vera hesitated, then continued in a warm motherly tone, "but don't you think it will be lonely? Someone as young and pretty as you shouldn't be living by herself way out in the country. . . ."

"I've never had a problem with loneliness," I lied.

Her eyes searched my face. "You're not alone then?"

I considered that information to be none of Vera's business and I didn't respond immediately. However, since it really wasn't important, it seemed childish not to answer. Finally I said, "I just don't mind being by myself; I'm really a very self-sufficient person."

"Oh." She laughed, a nervous little twitter; but she didn't cease her prying. "Did Stephen tell you how difficult it is to get good help out there? It's such a big house. . . ."

"I'm sure I'll be able to manage." I didn't tell her I couldn't afford hired help in any event. Then, hop-

ing to get her off the subject, I added, "Do you
know, I don't even know your last name, Vera."

"Oh, I'm sorry!" Color mounted in her cheeks. "I
just took it for granted . . . that's what comes of
living all one's life in a small town where everyone
knows everyone. It's Enders . . . Vera Enders."

I don't know why that bit of information came to
me as a shock. Automatically, I darted a quick look
at her left hand.

Vera did not pretend to ignore my reaction, and I
felt the warm blood staining my cheeks as she said,
"Stephen's my brother . . . and business partner."

"Oh," was all I could think of to say.

At that moment, our hostess rolled a flambé cart
up to our table and proceeded to prepare crêpes
suzette. Her hands, after adjusting the flame beneath the pan, moved quickly and deftly as her eyes
measured each step in the meticulous process: melting the butter, pouring the orange juice and Grand
Marnier, flipping and rolling the paper-thin pan-
cakes. Then, with a tilt of the pan, she set them
ablaze. Vera and I watched, fascinated, as blue
flames flared, danced, died. . . .

Our hostess now served up two plates, spooning
on the buttery orange sauce with a liberal hand,
then made her presentation with a grand flourish.
Vera and I clapped, smiled at each other, picked up
our forks and ate. Neither of us spoke another word
until we had licked our plates clean.

"That was absolutely perfect . . . everything was
delicious!" I had never spoken those words more
sincerely.

Visibly pleased, Vera replied, "I thought you
would enjoy this place, but"—she hesitated, then

added all in a rush—"I just can't believe you would enjoy living on Wiffen Cove. . . ."

I studied her face intently, considering again the possibility that it was she who had sent me the warning. I read nothing in her expression but concern. "Because you think I'd be lonely?"

"Not entirely. I just don't think it's safe for a woman alone to live in such an out-of-the-way place. There's always the danger of prowlers . . . you know the sort of world we live in today."

Her words brought a stab of unease. I remembered quite clearly Stephen saying they didn't have that kind of trouble on Saturday Island. Who was kidding who?

"And what if you got sick?" Vera rattled on, "I don't think there's even a telephone line out to that old place."

"It's very nice of you to be concerned, but, really, I'm not in the least afraid. I love the house. It's the kind of place I've always wanted. Besides," I added, the worry stamped on Vera's face making me feel a bit guilty, "I'll not be alone for long. I'll send for my three cats as soon as I'm settled!"

Vera sighed, spread her hands in a helpless gesture. "Well, you haven't moved in yet. Perhaps you'll change your mind."

Though I had had no intention of confiding in Vera, her concern seemed so genuine, I blurted out, "I've really nowhere else to go, Vera. I'm sure you know I inherited the house . . . I just can't afford to lose it."

Her expression did not change, but she gave her head a tired little shake and closed her eyes. When she opened them again, she asked, "When are you going to move in?"

"Well, I don't know . . . as soon as it can be arranged, I guess."

"Arranged?"

"Well, I want to have the place cleaned and a lot of Aunt Sylvia's things packed and stored. I'd really like to have someone come in and give me an appraisal. There's so much . . . of everything . . . in that house."

Vera's face brightened perceptibly. "That could take quite a while. Why don't you move into an apartment for now? It would be more comfortable for you, and certainly less expensive than the Sea Urchin Motel."

For some inexplicable reason, the suggestion brought me a sense of relief. Clearly, Vera was right about two things: it would be miserable trying to live in the house with workmen crawling all over, and a flat was bound to be less expensive than a motel. However, mindful of my ever-dwindling finances, I started to refuse, then I remembered the trust fund. Mr. Howell, my attorney, had indicated it could be mine as soon as I filed a letter of intent with respect to living in the House on Wiffen Cove. Then there would be the proceeds from all the stuff I intended to sell. . . .

"I know just the place," Vera offered eagerly.

So it was that by late afternoon I was settled in a small furnished flat overlooking the waterfront. The remodeled second floor of yet another old Victorian house, it consisted of three rooms: a small kitchen, a small bathroom, and a huge combination living, dining, and sleeping room. The upper half of the wall facing on the sea was set with diamond-shaped panes of leaded glass that turned the view into a patchwork quilt of water and sky and green-clad islands.

The furniture was old, but everything was lemon-fresh clean. The studio couch made into a surprisingly comfortable bed. A minuscule stone fireplace divided the outer wall into two equal halves. It was mostly for show—the heat was supplied by modern electric baseboard heaters. They struck an inharmonious note, but did keep the place cozy.

I was surprised at how pleased I felt to again have a place to call home, a place where I could fix my own morning coffee or late night snack whenever I felt in the mood. Not that I intended to do a lot of cooking. Nevertheless, before I went to bed that night, I visited the local market and came home with enough snacks and fast food to fill my few kitchen shelves to overflowing.

The next morning I rose early, started a pot of coffee to perking, and fixed myself a half a grapefruit. Then I put an egg on to soft boil and dropped an English muffin into the toaster.

It was after nine by the time I had finished my last cup of coffee, and I was just reaching for the phone when it rang. It was Stephen Enders. "I find I'll have to be out of the office most of the day," he said, "but I do want to help you as much as possible. Why don't we have dinner?"

I hesitated, then thought, why not? "All right. I . . ."

Enders, however, didn't wait for me to finish. "I'll pick you up at eight," he said and had hung up before I could even say good-bye. I was more surprised than irritated by his rudeness. To be truthful, I was pleased by the invitation even though I knew it was strictly business.

Actually, I couldn't imagine a real estate broker in Los Angeles taking a client out to dinner to discuss business—at least, not in a situation like this where no money was going to change hands. Or did Stephen Enders have something in mind at which I could not even guess? Come to think of it, had it truly been just the desire to be friendly, to meet someone new, that had prompted Vera's invitation? Did the two of them together have some ulterior motive?

Or was I just a suspicious big-city dweller? Obviously, life here on the islands was slower, the people friendlier, than I was used to. Besides, what ulterior motive could the Enderses possibly have?

While I mulled over these questions, I put away the breakfast things, then took a brisk walk along the strand. Back in the flat once more, I curled up with a book for the rest of the day, turning the last page about six o'clock. Then I took a long, hot bath with lots of bubbles and painted my nails a deep shade of crimson. As soon as my nails were dry, I slipped into the black, much-too-expensive sheer-wool dinner dress Emma had insisted I buy just before I left Los Angeles.

Dear Emma. When I had objected to the price, she said, "Money always goes, honey . . . if not for something you want, then for something you need. It's time you had something you *want*." How blessed I was to have so good a friend.

And while I was counting my blessings, I remembered to be grateful for the thick, curly, auburn hair that runs in my family. David always teased me about my "carrot top." It was his way of letting me know how much he cared. A lump rose in my throat and a wellspring of guilt bubbled up within me. How could I be dressing so carefully for an evening out with a man I scarcely knew when David . . .

Resolutely I blinked back the tears and tried to push the unhappy thoughts aside. It was over, I told myself. The past was past, and I couldn't change it. I was still struggling with myself when Enders arrived, promptly at eight.

Once we were settled in his car, he commented, "I hope you won't mind dining at Madelinne House again. It's the only place on the island where the food is good and the music"—he glanced at me and raised his eyebrow—"you *do* like to dance?"

I had to laugh. He had managed somehow to convey such grave concern with only a look. I didn't tell him it had been eight long years since I had been on a dance floor.

At Madelinne House, Stephen parked the car, killed the engine, then turned sideways in his seat to look at me. When he continued to gaze, unspeaking, that sense of vulnerability returned. I clutched nervously at my handbag and finally managed to say, "Penny for your thoughts."

"My thoughts are always worth more than a penny. . . ." A sardonic smile curled the corners of his mouth, then was gone so quickly I thought perhaps I had imagined it. His eyes softened, became warm and tender.

Something stirred deep inside me. Flustered, I snapped, "Sorry, but I'll not raise the bid!"

"That's probably a very wise decision." He winked, and reached for the door handle.

Once inside the restaurant, Stephen guided me toward a staircase that had eluded my notice on my first visit to Madelinne House. The main dining room, I now learned, was on the second floor. Large, with an open-beamed ceiling and a huge stone fireplace at one end, it too had a wall of glass overlooking the strait. Opposite the fireplace, seated to one side of a minuscule dance floor, a four-piece combo was tuning up.

The hostess greeted Stephen with a smile and showed us immediately to a table near the window, not too close to the dance floor. Stephen said, "I'll order for you if you like."

I hesitated, then nodded.

He smiled. "Good." Without a second glance at the menu, he proceeded to choose our dinner.

He must, I thought, eat here quite often. I also thought how good it was to have someone else make the decisions—even little ones. I had had to shoulder so much after the accident.

But that wasn't David's fault! Until the night of the accident, he had been the perfect husband—he would have been the perfect father. Dear David . . .

Stephen's voice startled me and I jumped. "I'm sorry," I stammered, "I . . . I was thinking. . . ."

"Not about me, obviously." There was pique in his tone.

I tried to smile. "You can't be sure about that, now can you?"

"Well, then, what were you thinking?"

Now I did smile. "Sometimes, my thoughts are beyond price."

Enders looked chagrined.

I continued quickly, not giving him a chance to speak, "But you were saying . . ."

He grinned good-naturedly. "I only asked if you like the flat. Are you all settled?"

"Snug as a bug. It's a charming place, and I feel quite at home already."

"Good. If you find you need anything, don't hesitate."

"Thanks very much, but Vera has taken care of everything. I just wish she didn't feel so strongly about my living at Wiffen Cove."

Stephen ignored my last remark, turning his head to stare out into the night. We sat in silence for a moment, then he turned back to me and smiled.

"Tell me about yourself."

"About me?" Suddenly I felt nervous and vulnerable again. "What do you want to know?"

"Oh . . . things like how you happen to be traveling by yourself. Are you still married?" The words were casual, but his eyes were watchful.

I could feel the hot blood again suffusing my cheeks. He's as nosy as Vera, I thought, feeling just a trifle irritated; but I found myself answering, "I'm traveling alone because it pleases me." I paused. "And . . . no, I'm not married any longer. I'm a widow."

The wine steward arrived and opened a bottle of cabernet sauvignon. Stephen sipped it, nodded, and the man filled our glasses. Stephen lifted his, smiled, and said, "To our mutual success, whatever the endeavor. . . ." And again that fleeting impression of cynicism brushed my mind.

We sipped the wine in silence for a while. Then Stephen remarked, "How do you plan to spend your time . . . way out there on Wiffen Cove?"

"I'm going to paint."

"Paint?"

I nodded.

His eyes considered me. "Houses? Portraits? Still lifes?"

"Oils, watercolors . . . I like to sit in the sun and paint whatever I see. I also do animal portraits."

"How do you get an animal to pose?"

"You don't," I confessed. "I do like to spend some time getting acquainted with the animal . . . observing it with its owner. But when I'm ready to begin painting, I get detail from snapshots."

"I'd like to see some of your work . . . may I?" Stephen's tone was sincere and I felt pleased.

"As soon as I'm settled," I promised.

The combo began to play and Stephen rose to his feet. "Let's dance," he said.

He was an excellent dancer, and it felt good to have a man's arms about me again, even in such a casual embrace. We didn't talk, just glided to the beat of the music, our bodies moving almost as one, around and around the tiny dance floor, oblivious to the other couples crowding about us. I looked up at Stephen and thought how handsome he was. He must have felt my gaze because he held me tighter for a fleeting moment, then released me as the music ceased.

The rest of the evening passed all too quickly. We talked and danced some more. The dinner was marvelous. I couldn't believe how late it was when Stephen looked at his watch and said, "They'll be closing soon. Let's go."

We were halfway down the staircase when we met another couple, a heavy-set young man and a tall blond woman wearing a gold lamé blouse. Her eyes were heavily made up as was her petulant mouth. The two men nodded and would have stepped around each other, but the woman reached out and grasped Stephen's arm.

"Whoa, Stevey, honey. Why you leavin' so early?" she drawled in a husky contralto. "Come on back an' Teddy'll buy you a drink." She swayed slightly, blinked her eyes, then fixed her gaze on me. "You, too, cutie. Don't let old Stevey here rush you into the sack too soon. . . ."

Stephen jerked his arm free of the woman's grasp and said to the man, "You'd better get her out of here, Ted, before she gets both of you in trouble." And without waiting for a reply, he hurried me down the stairs and out to the car. Before he unlocked the door and helped me in, he said, "I'm sorry about that little scene. Please . . . just forget it." That was all, no explanation of any kind. How strange, I thought, but I said nothing.

We didn't talk on the drive back to my flat. Stephen's attention seemed to be elsewhere, and I was undecided about asking him in for a nightcap. However, I need not have troubled myself because when we reached my door he said, "I'll not come in tonight."

So who asked you? I thought, irritated despite the sense of relief his words brought. But I smiled and said, "I enjoyed the evening. Thank you, Stephen."

He put my house key back in my hand, then placed a finger under my chin and raised my face to his. My heart began to pound and for one long agonized moment, I thought that he was going to kiss me.

But he only looked deep into my eyes. "I enjoyed the evening too. Call you tomorrow," he murmured. Then he was gone, running back down the stairs. At the foot, he paused and saluted me with a wave of his hand.

I waved back, then turned and went inside. My heart was still pounding as I closed the door behind me, and I couldn't help wondering what it would be like to be kissed by Stephen Enders. The next few weeks, I thought, smiling to myself, might be very . . . interesting. I had forgotten how much fun a mild flirtation could be.

But even as the words formed in my mind, the smile froze, the excitement faded. What right had I to be having fun while David lay cold in his grave? I knew the thought was irrational, yet try as I would, I could not shake the feelings of sorrow and guilt that followed me into my bed.

# FIVE

The sorrow that followed me to bed dissipated as I slept, and I wakened early the next morning filled with a sense of excitement and anticipation that I had not experienced in many a day. Tossing back the covers, I arose, stretched, then padded across the room to the kitchen, shrugging on my robe as I went.

The coffee was perking merrily and a muffin was warming in the toaster when I caught myself humming a happy little tune. I broke it off in the middle of a note, suddenly remembering Emma's oft-repeated admonition, "Sing before breakfast, cry before supper." I'm not superstitious, of course, but I saw no reason to tempt fate.

Nevertheless, the melody continued to dance round in my head and my feet kept time when I skipped down the stairs to retrieve the morning paper. Back in the flat, I filled an oversize mug with coffee, then curled up on the divan in front of the fireplace, and spread the paper open on my knees.

But instead of reading, I sat staring out the window. The sun, though not yet risen, streaked the morning sky with streamers of pink and pearl and gray, and edged the morning clouds with halos of fleeting glory. Awed by the shifting patterns of color and light, I held my breath, wondering if I would ever be able to capture that transient beauty with brush and paint.

Beginning with my very first day in kindergarten, I wielded a mean crayon. In high school I designed all the scenery for my senior class play and, when I entered college, it was as an art major. My teachers and local art critics all expected great things from me. I expected great things from myself.

But all that changed when I met David. At a Christmas party. It was a blind date, to be honest, arranged by one of my sorority sisters. As I said, for David and me, it was love at first sight. He looked at me and I looked at him, and suddenly there was no one else in the world. The only thing I remember about that Christmas party is the feel of David's arms about me, his lips on mine when he kissed me good night.

We were married the following June and I never returned to my studies. Did not, in fact, do much with my drawing or painting until after the accident. I was having too much fun setting up housekeeping, learning to cook, and loving my husband. Only when my darling was away, out in the field pursuing his career, did I sometimes set up my easel. . . .

I shivered as the happy memories dissolved before the dark shadows that now crowded to the surface of my mind. How late it had been, that terrible night, when David's plane finally landed; later still by the time we had picked up his luggage. And David was so tired. Though he tried to hide it, the circles under his eyes, the stubble on his chin, attested to the long hours he had spent living out of tents, often with no running water, hiking through rugged terrain, taking soil samples, performing measurements.

So I insisted on driving. Would things have ended differently if I had let David take the wheel?

Sitting there on the sofa, with the morning sun beaming in upon me, I was, nevertheless, lost in a memory so sharp, so real, I could feel my foot on the accelerator, see the darkness all about us as I edged the car up the ramp onto the freeway. Rain began to fall, only a heavy mist at first, then faster and faster, drumming on the roof and pelting against the windows. The road, in the glow of the headlamps, glistened wetly ahead. The windshield wipers swishswooshed gaily back and forth. We were all happy, so glad to have David safely home. His parents had been staying with me while David was away. He didn't want me to be alone.

Then it happened—that other car, hurtling across the meridian, the squeal of tires on wet cement, someone screaming, shrill, high-pitched, the agonized sound cut short by the shriek of rending metal. . . .

Somewhere in the street below, a car door slammed, the sound breaking my concentration. The memory dimmed. I opened my eyes. I was gripping the seat cushions so tightly my knuckles shone white. I forced myself to relax, releasing my breath in a long tremulous sigh. Everyone had agreed, the accident was not my fault. Nothing I might have done could have put us beyond the path of the other car.

That knowledge provided small comfort during

the weeks and months and years that followed when I thought of David's parents, who were killed that terrible night, of the baby I had lost. No comfort at all while I watched David's suffering, watched him wither a little more every day. I would rather it had been me! I tried to hide my own pain from him, but we knew each other so well. . . .

Without warning, another memory sent a shiver coursing through me: the first hospital bill. I could still remember the shock and the fear that had threatened to overwhelm me when I read the total due. The insurance was not nearly enough; and the other driver had no insurance, no property, no visible means of support. From that moment on, the specter of poverty had haunted us.

And always, day in—day out, I had lived with that awful unbearable feeling of guilt. Not that anyone, certainly not David, had ever so much as hinted that I was to blame. But I kept thinking, Why didn't I just stay home that night, let David take a taxi? If I had even stopped to buy a newspaper or something, it wouldn't have happened. Rationally, I knew I was being irrational; but the depression, the nightmares had been my constant companions for years.

It was Emma who suggested I start painting again. Dear Emma. Painting became my only escape from a world that suddenly held too much sorrow and pain and hopelessness. . . .

When I discovered that people were actually willing to pay me to paint portraits of their pets, it was a dream come true. For David and me animals and art were a shared passion. After the accident, when I began to do the pet portraits, David would sit in his wheelchair and watch, offering advice or criticism only when asked, but then doing so freely and with honesty.

I sighed, remembering, and a lump rose in my throat; tears threatened to spill over. I dashed them away with the heel of my hand. No! I thought, I will not let the past make me unhappy today.

I finished my coffee in a gulp, pushed the paper aside, and stood up. I had come to Saturday Island to paint, and paint I would. Moments later, dressed in a pair of faded blue jeans and a shapeless, paint-spattered sweater, I retrieved my easel, a canvas, and a box of paints from the back of my car. They made for an unwieldy load, but I managed to get everything across the street onto the strip of parkway opposite my flat.

I put everything down on one of the wooden benches while I looked first south and then west, considering the view. Imagine my surprise when I realized that when I looked west, I could actually see Wiffen Cove. Why, I thought, if one started immediately when the tide went out and did not dilly-dally along the way, one could easily walk from there to here on that narrow strip of rocky shore. However, as far as I could tell, there was no access from the parkway to the beach. I looked again at the wavelets gently lapping the shore and a tremor made its way down my spine. Even on a bright morning, the water looked black and forbidding, and again I thought, Woe to anyone caught on that strip of land when the tide begins to rise.

It was a morbid idea and I brushed it quickly aside. What I had to do at that moment was choose something to paint. The only likely subject, I decided, was that spear of granite thrusting up through the rippling waters of the strait to etch its image against the pale blue sky. The morning sun, slanting across the boulder's face, cast it in planes of bright light and deep, black shadow. Derelict logs floated about its base; seagulls floated and wheeled above.

I took a deep breath, reveling in the briny-sweet scent of seawater, then set to work. I had been painting steadily for perhaps an hour when I became aware that I had an audience. I stepped back and surveyed my efforts with a critical eye before glancing at the young couple who had settled down on one of the benches to watch. I smiled and the girl, at least, smiled back.

"What do you think?" I asked.

"It's pretty good . . ." the girl offered, "lots better than most."

"Oh, do lots of people paint along here?"

"Practically everyone, and they all try to paint the Tor."

I shrugged ruefully. "I had a feeling it might not be too original."

The girl nodded in sympathy. "But it's better than most . . . don't you think so, hon?" She turned to her companion, seeking concurrence.

The man shrugged. "Yeah," he muttered.

The girl glared at him, then turned back to me. "Well, I think it's very good!"

"Thank you," I said solemnly, repressing the urge to laugh.

They stood up, started to move off down the parkway. Then they stopped and engaged in a short, whispered conversation before turning back to me once more. The young woman took a deep breath, glanced up at her companion, then said, all in a rush, "Are you the lady who owns the House on Wiffen Cove?"

Now how, I wondered, did she know that, and why should she care? I didn't answer immediately. We stared at each other. The young woman's face flushed and she gave an uncomfortable wriggle. At last I said, "As a matter of fact, I do. Why do you ask?"

Again the woman glanced at the man as if for reassurance. He was staring at the ground with great concentration. "Well . . ." She hesitated, then blurted, "No reason, we just wondered."

"How did you know . . . ?"

But they were already moving rapidly away from me up the parkway.

I shrugged, thinking, Small towns! and went back to my painting. I didn't stop again until the sun had moved so high, the entire face of the Tor was shrouded in shadows. I put down my brushes and palette, wiped my hands on a rag I had tucked in my waistband, stretched, and looked around.

Only then did I notice the knot of people gathering in the parkway a block to the south. There was a tenseness about the group that was unmistakable. One woman was hurrying a reluctant child away across the road, all the while staring back over her shoulder. At the cliff's edge, a portly gray-haired man stood pointing downward, speaking with great animation to a gray-haired wraith of a woman who kept shaking her head and wringing her hands.

Curious, but undecided, I stood staring until the sound of a police siren rent the air. A moment later a squad car came barreling past, then screeched to a halt in the street behind the growing group of gawkers.

What was going on? Quickly, I thrust the brush I was holding into the turpentine, and started off at a trot, only to step on a loose stone and turn my ankle. Swearing under my breath, I hobbled over to the nearest bench, sat down, and started rubbing the offended joint.

But curiosity is a strong motivator. Despite the discomfort it caused, I limped back across the street, stowed my paints in the car, then made my way as quickly as I could up the street to join the throng. I went straight to the edge and looked over.

At first I saw nothing except the sweep of wet beach dotted with seaweed and driftwood. I looked farther out, my gaze tracing the edge of the receding tide until I saw it. A body. Head and shoulders wedged between two outcroppings of rock, legs twisted at an ungainly angle. A long strand of greenish-brown kelp had wound itself about the torso and the ends floated back and forth on the restless waters.

Another police car arrived and uniformed officers began herding the crowd back from the edge, urging people to go home, while a second group of officers hurriedly set up equipment in preparation for retrieval of the body. I didn't want to watch, but a sick fascination held me in thrall as they pulled it from between the rocks. My stomach lurched and I turned away, but not before I had had a clear view of the head, blond hair plastered in wet strips across the face. But it wasn't the face I recognized, it was the gold lamé blouse.

# SIX

My mind, like my stomach, was churning as I hobbled back across the street. The body on the beach. That long, blond hair. The lamé blouse . . .

The phone began to ring as I started up the stairs to my flat. Limping as fast as the pain in my twisted ankle would allow, I managed to reach the apartment, hop across the room, and pick up the receiver just in time to hear it click off at the other end. "Damn!" I said, and the word was uttered in pain as well as frustration.

I dropped the phone back into its cradle and glanced at my watch. One o'clock. I didn't feel hungry but I knew I should eat something. Once in the kitchen, however, I decided an ice bag for my ankle should take precedence. Filling a plastic bag with ice cubes and wrapping it in a towel took only a moment. Then I filled a bowl with cold cereal and sliced a banana over it. My thoughts continued to revolve about the dead woman. I was positive it was the same woman who confronted Stephen last night as we were leaving the Madelinne House. What was she—had she been—to Stephen Enders? Had there been some deeper meaning behind her vulgar comment to me?

I tipped some milk over the cereal, then carried the bowl back to the living room, but my mind never missed a beat. Did Stephen know the woman was dead—drowned there on the rocky shore? Had it been Stephen on the phone just now?

In an effort to shut out the unanswerable questions, I tried to read and when I couldn't keep my mind on the book, I tried to watch TV. But the memory of that lifeless body, garlanded in seaweed, kept worming its way into my mind. I even tried to write to Emma, but the ghost of that lifeless face veiled in pale strands of dripping hair kept insinuating itself between me and the sheet of paper.

When the phone rang again an hour or so later, I snatched it up, thankful for anything to distract my thoughts. I wasn't even disappointed when Vera's voice answered my hello.

"Stephen asked me to call," she said. "He had to leave on business very early this morning and didn't want to wake you. He'll be in touch when he returns." Her tone was cool, distant, not at all like her voice on the day we had gone to lunch.

I thanked her and hung up. The rest of the day was wasted in useless conjecture. Seeing the woman's body lying there among the moss-encrusted rocks had resurrected a number of unpleasant memories and I found myself wondering: How did Sylvia die? How did my sweater find its way to that hook above the car window that day at Wiffen Cove? Who had sent me that ridiculous note . . . ?

For the first time in the month since I had arrived on Saturday Island, I questioned the wisdom of moving into Aunt Sylvia's house. Still, I hadn't much choice. If I changed my mind now, I would have to repay the lump sum I had received from the trust fund. All the attorney had needed was my letter of intent to transfer the account to my name. Since the money had been accruing for over a year, it had been a considerable amount, a good part of which I had already spent. Besides, if I left Wiffen Cove, it would mean starting over in the business world, giving up my dream of becoming a painter.

No, I decided, I really haven't any choice. Anyway, what connection could there possibly be between that woman on the beach and Aunt Sylvia or me?

Then I told myself impatiently, Stop thinking about it. Thinking in circles never solves anything!

What I really needed was my daily walk along the parkway, but with that swollen ankle, that was out of the question. So I went to bed early, hoping to lose myself in sleep. But my eyes remained steadfastly open, my mind continued to whirl. When my bedside clock read twelve-thirty, I got up, took a sleeping tablet, and tried again.

I didn't wake until after nine the next morning. Groggy, gritty-eyed because of the sleeping pill, I crawled out of bed and staggered into the bathroom. Morning ablutions completed, I made my way to the kitchen to put on a pot of coffee before going down for the paper. Outside, the fresh salt air helped to clear my head and by the time I had climbed back up the stairs, I was feeling much better.

Saturday Island did not boast its own newspaper, and the drowning rated only a few paragraphs on an inside page in the *Seattle Times*. The article stated that the woman's name was Marjory Blake, that she was survived by a sister and a child. No mention was made of a husband. Death was deemed due to misadventure. According to the paper, it was believed she had gone for a walk along the parkway and somehow fallen over the edge in the dark. That was all the information given except for funeral arrangements.

I read the article twice. I don't know what I had expected it to say; but surely more than it did. Again I wondered about that encounter on the stairs. But, I thought, with a sudden burst of clarity, it's not what she meant by her crude remark, but what prompted it that should concern me. What had been Marjory Blake's connection with Stephen? I suspected it was one that Stephen was not proud of. Still, she had quite obviously been drinking. . . .

I looked at the article again, ". . . fallen over the edge in the dark." But she had been on her way upstairs with—what was his name? Teddy, that was it. We had seen her going upstairs with Teddy about one-thirty that morning. I sighed and shook my head. It was a dreadful thing—depressing.

I felt depressed and lonely once again. I wished the cats were there with me: Clarence, with his little pink nose and gravelly purr; Sheba, with her elegant calico coat and disdainful stare; and little Cleopatra, always chasing something—a ball, a butterfly, even a shaft of light. I swallowed the lump in my throat and took another disconsolate turn about the flat.

For a while, I toyed with the idea of calling Vera and asking her to lunch. However, I wasn't sure now I really wanted to press the friendship. There was something strange about Vera—I couldn't put my finger on it, but something about her bothered me. Perhaps, I thought, it was her sudden and inexplicable changes in attitude toward me—or did I just imagine it?

I was still debating the pros and cons of lunching with Vera when the phone rang. My heart jumped. Thinking it must be Stephen, I grabbed up the phone and said, "Hi!"

However, a crisp, feminine voice responded, informing me that my caller was Claire Moss, of Moss and Moss, Antiques and Objects d'Art. "I would like to speak with Ms. D'Ahl," she said.

"Kimberly D'Ahl speaking." I hoped the disappointment didn't register in my voice.

"How do you do, Ms. D'Ahl. Stephen Enders asked me to call. I understand you would like the late Ms. Belgedes's collection of antiques and art objects appraised."

"Oh," I said, momentarily taken aback, since my mind was cluttered with the morbid thoughts of the morning. Then, recalling my discussion with Stephen, I quickly added, "Thank you for calling. I do want the things appraised, and the sooner the better."

"Good! When can we get together to discuss arrangements?"

"Anytime you like . . . I'm free today."

Everything moved forward without a single hitch after that first meeting with Claire Moss. Before week's end, the appraisal was begun, and, to my chagrin, it soon became apparent that most of the art objects were only copies—very good copies, but copies nonetheless. Some of the larger pieces: the ballroom chandeliers, the bishop's chair, a few other items, were quite valuable; but even had I elected to sell everything, I would not have realized enough to make myself financially independent. I was disappointed. I had hoped we would find something: a Ming vase, a lost Rubens, or perhaps a black velvet bag full of uncut diamonds. . . .

The appraisal was a time-consuming process, but by mid-July everything had been catalogued, evaluated, and marked. Claire and Tom Moss were efficient and thorough. They even recommended dealers who would take on consignment all those things I did not wish to keep.

And all the other matters about which I had felt concern—plumbing, wiring, finding responsible gardeners, carpenters, and painters—were resolved with surprising speed and ease once Stephen returned. He handled all the details for me, and I found myself leaning on him far more than I had intended. It felt so good to have someone make decisions for me, shield me, worry about me.

Stephen had suggested, and I agreed, that it would be wise for me to wait until all the work had been completed before I actually took up residence in the House on Wiffen Cove. Since I had filed the letter of intent and the funds from the trust were now at my disposal, my cash position was much improved. In addition, I was certain to realize a considerable amount from the sale of all the things being offered through the dealers recommended by Claire and Tom. Not the fortune originals would have brought, but the copies were excellent and valuable in their own right.

So, what with one thing and another, it was the last week in August when I decided to fly back to

California, dispose of the few things I still had there, and bring the cats back to our new home. To this end, one sunny afternoon, I called Emma.

"How good to hear from you . . . we miss you, dear."

"And I miss you, Emma; but just wait till you see the house. It's a marvelous old mansion overlooking the Strait of Juan de Fuca. I even have my very own private beach!"

"Sounds wonderful. Have you moved in?"

"Not yet, but everything should be ready by the first of September. That's why I called. I'd like to fly back and spend a few days with you and Jerry, then bring the cats back up here with me. O.K.?"

"Anytime you say, Kimmy. Just let us know and we'll meet your flight."

"How are the cats? Do they miss me?"

Emma laughed. "Well they haven't lost any sleep or weight over it!"

"Sounds like it's time I brought them home . . . ungrateful twits!"

Emma sighed. "I'm going to miss them—almost as much as I miss you."

"Oh, Emma . . . you'll have to come visit soon as we're settled. You're all going to love the house . . . it's way out in the country with lots of trees and bushes. . . ."

I chattered on about the house and then we gossiped about some of our mutual acquaintances. Finally Emma said, "Remember to let us know when you are arriving and we'll be at the airport to meet you."

"Thanks, dear. I'll let you know."

"Bye, bye for now. . . ."

No sooner had I hung up the phone than it began to ring. When I answered, a very masculine voice said, "Hi, this is Marshall Thorne. I'd like to speak to Kimberly D'Ahl."

I hesitated, trying to place the name. I couldn't. "This is Kimberly D'Ahl. Should I know you, Mr. Thorne?"

"No, we've never met, but I was a friend of Sylvia Belgedes."

"Oh?" I waited, mystified.

"I'd appreciate a few minutes of your time."

I paused, unable to think of a good reason to say either "yes" or "no."

"I could stop by right now if it would be convenient." The voice was pleasant.

"Why? I mean, since I don't know you, Mr. Thorne . . ."

"It's about the house . . . would today be convenient?"

Still I hesitated, but his mention of Aunt Sylvia intrigued me and I heard myself saying, "Actually, I have nothing special to do right now if you'd like to stop by. . . ."

He repeated my address and added, "I'll be there in ten minutes."

Automatically, I began to straighten the room: I folded up the morning paper, puffed a pillow, then picked up my luncheon tray and carried it out to the kitchen. I was in the bathroom combing my hair when the clatter of the door knocker announced my visitor.

I went to open the door. A stocky man with unruly brown hair stood on the landing. His smile was quick and warm, but intuitively I noted the sadness lurking in his wide-set dark eyes. "I'm Marshall Thorne," he said, and his voice, too, was pleasant and warm.

"How do you do?" I opened the door wide and stepped aside. "Won't you come in?"

We stood for a moment, observing each other, and I had the strangest feeling we had met before. I felt certain he sensed it too.

He stepped inside and glanced about the room before moving over to stare out the window. "Great view. . . ."

"It is beautiful, isn't it?"

He turned back. Our eyes met. Again, for a long moment we stared at one another, and the quiet in my little flat held us close.

I broke the silence. "Won't you sit down . . . ?"

He moved toward the chair I indicated. I sat down facing him across a low oak coffee table and tucked my feet up under me.

"Now, what is it you wish to discuss with me?"

He seemed in no hurry to answer. The trace of a smile lurked about the corners of his mouth, but those dark mournful eyes were filled with shadow. A silence, mellow and full of peace, lay between us.

"I lived on Saturday Island when I was a kid. . . ." He paused, laughed self-consciously. "I always admired the House on Wiffen Cove."

Again the silence settled upon us. Finally I said, "Is that what you wanted to tell me?"

He shifted uncomfortably in his chair and his gaze wandered away, across the room, as he spoke. "Well, what I really wanted was to buy the house."

"It's not for sale."

He sighed, drummed his fingers on the arm of the chair. "I thought it couldn't hurt to ask."

"No, it never hurts to ask," I agreed; but silently I wondered why he had come to me to inquire about the place. Why hadn't he gone to the realtor? How had he known I was the new owner?

In the silence that followed, his gaze returned to me, fixed itself on my face, but he wasn't seeing me. Thoughts churned behind his eyes, such nice brown eyes. He wasn't exactly handsome, but he had a pleasant face—good strong jaw, nice straight nose, broad forehead beneath sun-bleached brown curls. Probably older than he looks, I thought.

Suddenly he smiled. "I understand Sylvia Belgedes was your aunt."

I almost rolled my eyes heavenward. Did everyone on this island know all about me? However, I replied politely, "As a matter of fact, she was my husband's aunt."

"Oh," he said, looking surprised. Then he added, "I guess I should have asked to speak to Mr. D'Ahl. . . ."

I shook my head. "It's all right," I said, "I'm a widow. I inherited the place from my husband."

He considered that bit of information, apparently decided condolences were not in order. Instead he asked, "Did you know Ms. Belgedes well?"

"I didn't know her at all . . . neither did my husband, really. It was a complete surprise when we learned she had left him the property."

"It's a funny world." Thorne shook his head. "Do you know, soon as I heard that Ms. Belgedes had died, I decided to buy the place. It never occurred to me that she might have relatives." He stopped, colored slightly, then added quickly, "I'm sorry . . . it's just that she had been a recluse for so many years . . . even when I was a kid, there was talk . . ." His voice dwindled into embarrassed silence.

"What kind of talk, Mr. Thorne?" I sat forward, searching his face with my eyes.

He shifted uneasily in his chair. "Oh, it was nothing, really . . . just small-town gossip. . . ."

I gave him an encouraging smile. "It's all right, Mr. Thorne. My husband told me his aunt was sort of a . . . well, free spirit. Born thirty years too soon, as they say."

He nodded, but his eyes . . . those dark, sad eyes . . . held a guarded look.

"Tell me," I said, "how did you meet Aunt Sylvia? Did you like her?"

Marshall Thorne sighed, settled a little deeper into his chair. "How did I meet Sylvia? Well, I must have been about eight or nine . . . a couple of my friends dared me to knock on Sylvia's door. She caught me! Liked to have scared me stiff. When she invited me in and offered me some tea, I was afraid to say no." He laughed, and there was real affection in the sound.

He had been staring out the window as he spoke. Now he returned his attention to me and when our eyes met, again that feeling of *déjà vu* swept over me. I knew he felt it too; I could sense the response in him. I was the first to glance away. He stood up and walked over to the fireplace and, when I again raised my eyes, he was watching me, his expression thoughtful.

Finally I asked, "How well did you get to know Aunt Sylvia?"

"Pretty well, actually. She used to ask me over for lunch, or we would walk in the garden or go down to the beach. I liked her . . . it was always easy to talk to her. She made me feel important." He stopped, laughed, shook his head. "Well, I was just a kid, just beginning to realize girls are different from boys . . . and Sylvia was a very beautiful young woman."

I felt a stab of remembrance. David had said almost the same thing: ". . . the prettiest woman . . . and she always smelled good."

While we talked, clouds had been massing along the horizon, and now they were moving inland at a rapid pace, blocking out the sky, dimming the sun's light. A stiff wind came roaring in across the strait, whipping the black water into a froth, bending the boughs of the stunted trees along the bluff. A flash of lightning lit the sky and the first drops of rain splattered against the windowpanes.

"How about a cup of coffee . . . or tea?" I suggested.

"Coffee sounds great . . . if it's not too much trouble."

"No trouble at all . . . I'd like some, too."

I went to the kitchen filled the coffee pot, and plugged it in. Next I retrieved the large pewter tray I had found in one of the cupboards and loaded it with cups, spoons, and napkins together with a sugar bowl, creamer, and plate on which I arranged an assortment of cookies. The coffee was ready by then and I filled the cups before carrying the tray into the living room and placing it on the coffee table.

I handed one of the steaming cups to Thorne, who promptly added cream and a heaping spoonful of sugar. Then he loaded the saucer with cookies and sat back smiling broadly.

"Smells great," he remarked, taking a deep whiff of the steam rising from the cup. "Thanks."

We sat in silence for a while. My guest munched his cookies and I watched. David had always put cream and a heaping spoonful of sugar in his coffee. After the accident, coffee in the evening had become a ritual. It was one of the few luxuries we had allowed ourselves. I bought a special blend of dark roast beans with chicory and sometimes we added cardamon, sometimes cinnamon or chocolate.

The rain was streaming down the windows now, and the pounding of the storm-lashed water could be heard above the moaning of the wind. Thorne set his cup back on the tray and I asked, "Refill?"

He hesitated, glanced at his watch, then shook his head. "That was good coffee, thanks; but I should be going."

I smiled.

"About the house . . . if you should decide to sell . . ."

I was shaking my head vigorously, and his voice trailed away. He sighed, started to reach for another cookie, changed his mind. I had the distinct feeling there was something else he wanted to say. Slowly he rose to his feet. Still he lingered and an impish smile tilted a corner of his mouth. "Well . . ." he said slowly, "if I promise to tell you everything I know about Sylvia, do I have an open invitation to at least visit Wiffen Cove from time to time?"

"If that's your price for the information"—I spread my hands in a helpless gesture—"what can I say?"

We both laughed.

"That helps." Thorne sighed. "If I can't have the house, at least I've secured visiting privileges."

Although his tone was rueful, I thought I also detected a trace of something else in his voice. Relief, perhaps . . . or was it satisfaction?

I, too, rose to my feet and walked with him to the door. It wasn't until I opened it and we saw the rain sluicing from the roof in sheets that I realized just how hard it was raining. I closed the door again. "You can't go out in that . . . you'll be soaked!"

"My car's right down there on the street," he said doubtfully.

"I know what," I said. "Wait a minute." I went over to the closet and pulled out my old plaid umbrella. "Take this . . . I never use it."

"Are you sure?"

"It won't keep you completely dry, but it will help . . . go on, take it."

In the end, he accepted the umbrella and left, keeping close under the eaves until he reached the foot of the stairs. From there, he bolted across the street and into his car. He flashed his headlights a couple of times in farewell, then pulled slowly from the curb and drove off down the street.

I didn't go inside immediately but lingered in the open doorway, breathing in the freshness of the newly washed air, feeling the misty spray thrown up as the pelting rain spilled from the eaves.

Marshall Thorne. The name repeated itself in my mind. Why, I wondered, had Marshall Thorne come to call on me? That was something I intended to find out. I didn't for one minute believe he really wanted to buy the House on Wiffen Cove.

# SEVEN

Stephen took me to dinner the night before I left for California. We rode the ferry to the mainland, then drove up the coast to a seafood restaurant where the salmon was broiled over an open pit and the salad bar boasted iced lobster, crab, and shrimp. We sat at a window table overlooking the channel and Stephen ordered a bottle of champagne. When the waiter had filled our glasses, we drank a toast to the House on Wiffen Cove.

"Because it brought us together," Stephen smiled.

Then we drank a toast to Aunt Sylvia. "Because it was her house," we said in unison, laughing. I added quickly, "I really am very grateful to Aunt Sylvia. The house . . . the income . . . I only wish I had known her . . . could have thanked her in person. . . ."

Outside, dusk was deepening into night. High overhead, the first starshine flickered. On the channel, where there had been boats, now only disembodied lights floated to and fro. A busboy approached, lighted the candle in the miniature hurricane lamp on our table, then withdrew. A sudden burst of raucous laughter at the next table shattered the quiet.

Stephen spoke. "How long do you plan to be gone?"

"Ten days. I'll be back a week from Saturday."

"Anything I can do for you while you're away?"

I considered the question. "Like what did you have in mind?"

"Whatever."

"Well, if it wouldn't be too much bother . . . I'd really appreciate it if you could check on the workmen and the house while I'm gone."

"Consider it done."

Our conversation was interrupted by a round of applause announcing the entrance of the evening's entertainer, a chubby young comedian who did a take-off on Hamlet's soliloquy: "To eat or not to eat . . . is that the question?" We sipped our champagne, laughing, exchanging companionable glances from time to time.

How was it, I wondered, that Stephen and I had slipped so quickly, so easily, into such a comfortable relationship? Probably, I decided, because I'm so alone here, and he has been so considerate, so helpful.

While his attention was on the entertainer, I studied Stephen's face through lowered lashes. He was easily the handsomest man I had ever known, and he was exciting . . . a fact with which I was not entirely comfortable. I had spent too many years fighting the kinds of feelings he awoke in me.

It hadn't been easy after the accident. David was my first, my only lover. One of my dearest memories is of our wedding night. How tender, how caring of my innocence he had been; how slowly he had awakened my passion, waiting until I wanted him as much as he wanted me. Then how gently he had taken me. . . .

During that first year of our marriage I had learned to know his beautiful, vibrant body as well as I knew my own. We never tired of one another, could never have enough of each other. Night after night I lay in the circle of his arms, exulting in the feel of his hands, his lips, caressing me, thrilling me, driving me almost wild with desire until together we were swept into a maelstrom of ecstasy and fulfillment.

Then, in the twinkling of an eye, it was all snatched from us. For months my body ached for his. But as time passed, we learned to accommodate; we learned how to comfort without arousing desire. But it hadn't been easy. . . .

My reverie was broken by a round of applause that followed the entertainer off the floor, and my thoughts were back in the present when Stephen turned to me once more. "What did Marshall Thorne have to say?"

The question caught me by surprise. "Thorne? Oh, Thorne," I said. "Goodness, I'd almost forgotten."

That wasn't entirely true, of course. The meeting with Marshall Thorne had stirred something in me —something I couldn't quite put my finger on. I found myself thinking of him at odd times, wondering about him in a most unexpected way.

Stephen was toying with the salt cellar, sliding it back and forth between his thumb and little finger. The diamond in his onyx ring flashed and blazed.

After a long moment, he raised his eyes, looked at me, but said nothing.

"Well, let me think. . . ." I knitted my brows, chewed on my thumb. Stephen did not smile, and for a moment something hard and cold glinted in his eyes. Surprised, I asked, "Is it so important?"

"Probably not." His tone was noncommittal, but he continued to watch me intently.

Suddenly I felt a twinge of irritation. Was he checking up on me? But that was ridiculous. Why would he? With a shrug, I answered, "Nothing much. He wanted to buy the House on Wiffen Cove . . . said he knew Aunt Sylvia. Why?"

Stephen straightened up. "No reason . . . just curious." Abruptly he leaned forward, reached across the table, and covered my hands with his. "Maybe I'm jealous." His eyes searched my face and my heart began to beat faster. His fingers tightened about mine. "You're a very desirable woman. . . ."

I was disconcerted by the sudden tide of passion his touch unleashed—sensations and yearnings I had thought long since buried and forgotten. Now, sitting there, my pulses pounding, the touch of Stephen's fingers sending tiny shock waves up my arms, I found myself wondering what it would be like to have him make love to me. And the very thought unleashed another rush of heat.

Mercifully, at that moment the waiter arrived with our food. Stephen released my hands and I quickly slid them into my lap to hide their trembling. When I again looked at Stephen, he was gazing out the window once more, his face in profile, serene and remote.

The waiter departed. Stephen turned back to me and smiled. If he had been aware of my feelings, he gave no clue. We ate slowly, talked lightly of inconsequential things, lingered late over our coffee. It was close to eleven o'clock when we left the restaurant and drove back to the ferry.

During the return trip we stood on deck, leaning against the rail. Moonlight brushed the dark waters of the strait with glittering silver, turned the boat's wake into a ribbon of gleaming white satin. The water whispered against the hull. But Stephen remained withdrawn—didn't even put his arm around me, a circumstance that I found at once disappointing, yet reassuring. I wasn't at all certain how I felt about this man, he was so unlike any other I had ever known . . . older, more sophisticated. The physical attraction was undeniable, but . . .

The ferry docked; we returned to Stephen's car. It was very late when we pulled to a stop at the curb in front of my flat. Stephen opened the gate and we walked up the path, climbed the stairs in silence. I handed him my keys; he unlocked the door.

"Would you like another cup of coffee . . . or perhaps a nightcap?" We were standing close together on the small landing, and I looked up into his face as I spoke.

He didn't answer. Instead, he put his arms about me, kissed me, his lips gentle on mine. I slipped my arms about his neck and clung to him, savoring the warmth of his embrace. His arms drew me closer, his kiss grew more passionate. Abruptly he released me. His voice was husky when he whispered, "Do you want me . . . to come in?"

I was trembling. I did want him to come in . . .

wanted him. But the years of conditioning were too strong. I shook my head. My voice, too, held a tremor as I whispered, "Perhaps it would be wiser to call it a night."

His fingers brushed my hair, caressed my cheek. "Are you sure?"

I nodded, but I did not draw away from him and he bent his head, kissed me again before he said, "I'll drive you to the airport in the morning. Be ready at six."

It wasn't until I was curled snug and safe in my bed that I began to wonder, How had Stephen known about Marshall Thorne's visit?

On the plane to Los Angeles, the next day, my thoughts kept returning to Stephen, to the evening just past. Did he really think I was desirable? Had he been just a bit jealous of Thorne? And what did I really feel for Stephen? He was so handsome, so exciting. . . .

And then I felt guilty. How, a small voice inside me asked, can you be so attracted to another man, so stirred by another man's touch, when David . . . ?

Stung by that small voice, I suddenly felt angry. Was it not enough that I had loved David dearly? Had I not been a true, faithful wife to the very end? And, I thought, Now it's over; he's gone!

Because of you, whispered that wretched little voice. He's gone. . . .

"And he's never coming back!" The words were past my lips before I could catch them. Embarrassed, I turned to look out the window, hoping no one had heard my outburst; but my thoughts continued to run in circles until the plane touched down at Los Angeles International.

The ten days with Emma and Jerry flew by. I told Emma about Stephen, how thoughtful he had been, how he made me feel.

"It's time you knew a little fun and laughter, honey. Enjoy yourself," she said. Then added, "Just don't rush into anything you can't easily get out of."

When I boarded the plane for the flight home, Clarence, Cleo, and Sheba were with me. The trip was uneventful and we landed at Sea-Tac International right on time. Stephen was there, waiting for me. At sight of him, I could feel the excitement beginning to build inside me, and I had to acknowledge that I had missed him more than I cared to admit, even to myself.

He gave me a warm hug and a kiss on the cheek, then drew back to look down into my face. "You look wonderful! No wonder I've missed you."

"I missed you, too," I said, then turned away, suddenly self-conscious.

"Give me your claim checks," he said. "We'll go get your luggage."

I had warned Stephen when he offered to meet my plane that I would be accompanied on my return by the three cats.

"Not to worry," he had said airily.

He had not spoken idly. I laughed when I saw the vehicle in which he came for us: a station wagon that could easily have handled three Great Danes.

"As a matter of fact," Stephen admitted, "I borrowed this behemoth from a neighbor who has three Great Danes and six kids."

He put my suitcase and the Port-a-Pet in the back.

The three cats, who had been sedated for the flight, were still sleeping peacefully.

Every day that I was away, I had thought about Stephen; but now that we were together again, I felt shy and subdued. I was aware of a certain restraint in Stephen, too. All during the long trip back to Saturday Island, conversation was superficial. I didn't even think to ask about Vera until we were nearing Wiffen Cove.

"She's fine." Stephen gave me a quick sidelong glance and added, "She's still not too happy about you living way out here alone."

For the first time, it struck me as odd that Vera should be so concerned while Stephen was not. Was she right? Was it dangerous for me to live way out there alone? If Stephen really cared about me, why wasn't he worried about me? An unexpected twinge of disappointment and hurt followed the thought.

I watched the thick undergrowth slide by, at the same time aware of the boughs of the trees above us, closely entwined, blotting up the bright noontide light, leaving the road beneath in eternal gloom. I shivered.

"Cold?"

As if you cared! I thought childishly.

Just then we drove over the crest of the hill and the house came into view. I caught my breath in delight, my worrisome thoughts forgotten. "Oh, Stephen, it is beautiful!"

The carpenters and painters had wrought a small miracle. Gone were the sagging shutters, the broken railings, the fallen bits of gingerbread. Everything was in its place, and the beige paint I had chosen glowed warm and clean in the sun's rays.

The grounds, too, had undergone a remarkable transformation: The newly mown lawn was a carpet of green; in the flower beds, transplanted pansies, marigolds, lupine, and iris, together with many plants I could not name, blossomed. The undergrowth along the brow of the hill above the cove had been removed, providing a clear view of the strait, which, at that moment, was dotted with an armada of tiny boats, white sails billowing.

I had arranged for a gardener to mow the lawn and weed the flower beds, but I had not expected anything like this. In dismay, I turned to Stephen. "It's wonderful, but I didn't order all this . . . I just can't afford . . ."

He reached over and patted my hand. "Don't worry about the expense. This job didn't cost nearly as much as you might imagine. There are always men, here on the island, in need of a job." As he spoke, Stephen pulled the car to a stop under the porte cochere and we got out.

Before we unloaded the car, I stood for a moment, gazing about, and tears gathered in my eyes. It's mine! I thought—really mine.

"Something the matter?"

I shook my head. I couldn't tell Stephen how I felt —I didn't understand it myself. It was as if I had come home after a long absence. "Let's hurry," I said, "I can't wait to see the inside."

We carried my luggage and the cats, still dozing in their Port-a-Pet, into the kitchen. Then Stephen insisted we take a quick tour of the house. At first, I thought everything was as I remembered it. Then, in the parlor overlooking the rose garden, I found the Queen Anne rocker and piecrust tier table, that had belonged to my mother, sitting in the bow window. And as we moved from room to room, I found other odds and ends of furniture I had shipped from California: an ornate oriental chest that had belonged to David's grandfather was standing near the fireplace in another sitting room. The cat pole, a large and very handsome affair with numerous hidey-holes and ledges where the cats could play and sleep and sharpen their claws, had been set up in a room across the hall from the kitchen.

I stopped, turned to Stephen. "Thank you," I said. "Everything is exactly where I'd have chosen to put it."

He leaned forward, brushed a kiss across my lips. "If you are pleased, I'm happy."

We returned to the kitchen then, retrieved my suitcase, and went upstairs. In the large front bedroom, someone had made up the four-poster, and on a low table in the alcove, there was a huge old-fashioned bouquet of snapdragons, daisies, carnations, and stock. I turned to Stephen, more thanks trembling on my lips; but he was staring at the bouquet, obviously as surprised as I.

Looking at the flowers once more, I discovered a card tucked down amid the blossoms. On it, in a crisp, clear script was written: "Welcome Home!" It was signed: "Marsh Thorne." I slipped the card into the pocket of my cardigan and turned to face Stephen once more. "They're from Marshall Thorne."

Stephen's left eyebrow quirked upward, but he made no comment.

"How do you suppose he got them up here?"

Stephen shook his head. "I've no idea unless he

came yesterday while the window washers were still at work."

I leaned toward the blossoms hoping for a whiff of fragrance. "How beautiful they are," I sighed. "How thoughtful of him."

However, when I looked back at Stephen I had to laugh, his chagrin was so obvious; and I made haste to add, "But most of all, I'm grateful for your help. Everything looks beautiful, Stephen. Thank you." I walked back to him and placed a small kiss at the corner of his mouth.

Mollified, he asked, "Now what do you want to do?"

"Well, I'll have to go back to town to get my car." I glanced around the room once more. "But I guess I could move in tonight. I'll need my things from the apartment. . . ." I looked at my watch. It was almost one o'clock. "Maybe I'd better spend tonight in town. Then I'll have plenty of time tomorrow to move the rest of my things out here, get some supplies for the larder. . . ."

A grin was spreading over Stephen's face. "Why don't you check the kitchen before you decide," he suggested, looking, as my mother would have said, like the cat that swallowed the canary.

"You mean that's all been taken care of . . . ?"

"Remember Helen Riley?"

I nodded. "The young woman from the motel . . ."

"You mentioned you'd want someone who could help from time to time. She's an excellent worker; I know because she cleans for Vera. I gave her the job of airing this place and unpacking for you."

"Bless you! That's wonderful." I stopped, a vision

of my bank balance flashing before my eyes. "But, Stephen . . . I really can't afford . . ."

He held up a hand. "Not to worry. I told you. People out here on the island don't expect an arm and a leg like they do in the big cities. O.K.?"

I shook my head, but I smiled.

"Now, there's something I want you to do for me." Stephen's face had become serious.

"Anything I can. . . ."

He laughed. "Let me take you to lunch . . . I'm hungry!"

Moonlight, spilling through the mullioned glass in the alcove windows, covered the walls and ceiling with squares of brightness.

The silence pulsing in my ears kept time with the thudding of my heart. It's too quiet, I thought. Something must be wrong with David; and even as the idea began to form, I was up, and halfway across the room searching for his bed before I remembered. David was gone and I was alone, spending my first night in the House on Wiffen Cove. I stopped, took a deep breath, held it, listening. What had wakened me? Had I been dreaming? Yes. That was it. I had been dreaming . . . someone was calling me . . . someone . . . I shook my head. I couldn't remember.

But now I was wide awake. I glanced at the digital clock on my nightstand—2:27 A.M. I shivered, the chill of early morning seeping into me. What I need right now, I decided, is a glass of warm milk and honey to comfort me. And still I hesitated, cowed by my childish fear of the darkness that waited just beyond my bedroom door.

And try as I would, I could not keep my thoughts from returning to the previous evening. I had retired early, seeking the sanctuary of the big front bedroom where I could lock the door behind me.

Not that I'm afraid, I had assured myself. But whose imagination wouldn't play them tricks, alone in a house as big as this? Besides, it's only natural for a person to be nervous the first night in a new place. Just go to bed, I told myself. You'll feel better tomorrow.

Now, standing there in the moon-washed darkness, I tried not to remember that from the moment I had returned to Wiffen Cove the previous afternoon and walked into the house, I was obsessed by the feeling that I was not alone; that someone else, someone who moved, silent and invisible, listening and watching, shared the place with me.

And the cats had been less than a comfort. The three of them prowled about the downstairs rooms, nervous and ill-at-ease, sniffing in the corners, leaping up onto the windowsills to gaze with woe-filled eyes at the unaccustomed landscape.

After dinner, Clarence and Cleo had started a halfhearted game of tag up and down the cat pole, but they soon gave it up and came to snuggle beside me in a large, lumpy, wingback chair.

Sheba had managed to open one of the glass doors in a huge breakfront bookcase and draped herself gracefully along one of the upper shelves. There she dozed, fitfully, opening her eyes from time to time to stare intently at nothing. And each time I began to relax, she lifted her head and uttered a mournful "Maaoouu," raising not only the hair on the back of my neck, but my backside half out of my chair.

By nine o'clock I had had enough. "Well, my darlings," I said to the three, "I've had it! Let's retire to the bedchamber." I picked up Cleo and walked out into the hall calling over my shoulder, "Come on, Sheba, Clarence . . . let's go . . . beddy-bye time."

Sheba stood up, stretched, jumped to the floor, and sat down. Clarence gave his whiskers a few swipes with his paw and Cleo snuggled down against my shoulder purring softly. "Come on," I coaxed, moving slowly up the hall. Sheba stood up and, tail held tall and straight above her back, began to move sedately toward the door. Just as she started through, Clarence went into action. Giving a mighty leap, he almost bowled her over as he raced by and up the hall ahead of me.

Sheba hissed and grumbled—I scolded, "Shame on you Clarence. Sheba is an old lady. You shouldn't tease her that way."

Somehow we all reached the stairway together. I started up, still carrying Cleo and watching the other two out of the corner of my eye. I had tripped over one or another of them too many times. I didn't relish a tumble down the stairs now. Especially when I'm all alone and way out here—the thought flashed through my head.

I was about halfway up the staircase when Cleo suddenly began to writhe in my grasp; she dug her claws into my shoulder, and leaped down. The hair on her back stood up and her tail fur was fully extended. She raced back down the steps and jumped completely over Clarence and Sheba, who were crouched at the bottom, hissing and snarling. Their eyes, enormous black pools filled with yellow and red fire, were fixed on something at the top of the stairs.

My heart froze, then began to pound. The cats had fled. I would have run, too, but my legs wouldn't move. I leaned against the wall to keep from collapsing, while my mind raced. I have long been convinced that cats are psychic. Everyone knows they can hear sounds humans can't hear, see things humans can't see. Had Cleo, Sheba, and Clarence detected something I could not? I forced myself to look up the stairway, to search the darkness above. I could see nothing. Nothing moved, no sound disturbed the silence. And still I stood, staring upward into the darkness, my heart thudding against my ribs while fear held me entwined in its clammy embrace.

Slowly I became aware that my shoulder, where Cleo had buried her claws in her efforts to escape, felt as if it were on fire. I took a deep breath, reached up, and began to rub. As some modicum of commonsense returned, I assured myself, You're letting your imagination run away with you. You know Cleo is afraid of her own shadow. It was probably her antics that scared Sheba and Clarence.

I took a firm grip on the banister and continued upward, all the while explaining to myself that it was the long trip, the new and strange surroundings that had upset the cats. But I couldn't dispel the sense of foreboding, and I walked through every room on the second floor, even looked in the closets and behind the shower curtains before I retired to my bedroom, carefully locking the door behind me.

Once safely tucked in, I tried to read for a while but I was uncomfortable sitting up in bed in the lighted room with the windows undraped—the old curtains had been removed by the window washers, and the new ones I had ordered were not yet ready. I knew that no one could possibly see in, still I felt uncomfortable. It was not yet ten o'clock when I turned off the light and settled down to sleep.

But now, at two twenty-seven in the morning, I was wide awake, and I wanted a glass of warm milk and honey. So go! I told myself. You can't let yourself give in to a lot of foolish fears.

With something less than joyful enthusiasm, I turned on the lights and started down. But I had taken only a few steps before I stopped again, remembering that there was no covering over the kitchen windows either. To provide a sense of security, I had tacked sheets over the windows in the room where the cats and I had spent the evening, but the windows in the kitchen, like those in my bedroom, remained bare.

I half-turned, ready to rush back to the bedroom. Again I stopped. See here, you gutless wonder—I borrowed that phrase from some Marine Corps movie I had seen—if you give in to this foolishness, you'll never be happy in this house. Now, damn it, go on down to the kitchen and get that glass of milk!

With a new sense of bravado, I continued down the stairs and into the kitchen. The cats were there, curled close together in the Port-a-Pet. When I turned on the light, they all opened their eyes, and Clarence rolled over onto his back and stretched. I poured some milk and a spoonful of honey into a pan and set it on the stove, then filled a bowl with milk for the cats and put it on the floor.

Slowly, my courage began to reassert itself. However, when my milk was warm, I poured it quickly into a glass and carried it, posthaste, back upstairs to my room. After locking the door and turning off the light, I walked over to the alcove, sank down on the cold, bare wood of the window seat and tucked one leg beneath me. How nice it will be, I thought, when the new cushions and drapes are in place.

I sipped my milk, listened to the silence, and stared down into the empty garden below. In the moonlight, the whole world was black and white. Those objects that were familiar and reassuring in the light of day assumed a vague and alien air in the moon's surreal glow. And as I watched, amid the black shadows cast by the trees at the garden's edge, blacker shadows seemed to form, to move, to flow, one into another, only to separate again in a slow, lugubrious dance.

A thrill of fear moved along my spine as I leaned forward, straining my eyes, trying to assure myself that it was only an illusion, a trick of the moonlight, of my imagination. Surely no one would be out there on the cliff! What would they be doing? And yet, I could almost make out a figure—or was it two figures? The silence pressed against my eardrums and my eyes hurt with the effort to see more clearly. The moon slid down the sky, predawn blackness enveloped the world, and yet I sat, huddled in the corner of the alcove, my forehead pressed against the glass.

Sunlight brushing my eyelids wakened me. Cold and stiff, I still sat in the alcove, my leg twisted under me. The yard below was empty as was the area under the trees. I glanced at the clock; it said 5 A.M. I tried to stand up, but the leg that had been tucked up under me on the ledge had gone to sleep and I stumbled, almost knocking over Marsh's bouquet. Muttering a string of expletives, I tottered back to bed.

The ringing of my front doorbell wakened me the second time that morning. Bleary-eyed, I squinted into the brilliant sunshine that filled the room, fervently wishing that whoever was at the door would go away. But the strident bell was insistent. At last, in desperation, I rose, pulled on my robe, and padded down the stairs, grumbling to myself about the stupidity of having the front doorbell circuited to ring in the bedchamber. I had almost reached the end of the hall when I remembered I had not stopped to comb my hair. *C'est la vie,* I thought, and opened the door.

There, leaning jauntily on my old plaid umbrella, a crooked grin on his boyish face, stood Marshall Thorne.

# EIGHT

My eyes, in a quick reflex motion ran down his body, taking in the broad shoulders, the sunbrowned, muscular thighs clad in shorts. I swallowed and blinked my way back to his face.

"Good morning," he said. "I just happened to be in the neighborhood . . ."

I don't know whether I was more surprised to see him, or embarrassed to have him see me, hair disheveled, clutching a faded, shapeless flannel robe about my person. "Please . . ." I said, "take a slow turn around the garden, then ring the bell again," and I closed the door, not waiting for him to reply.

I ran back upstairs, washed my face, brushed my teeth, combed my hair, and slipped into a pair of jeans and a T-shirt before racing back down just as the bell again filled the house with its clamor. I pulled the door wide.

Thorne stepped inside and offered me the umbrella. "Thought I better return this before another storm blows in. I really appreciated your lending it to me. That was one wet afternoon!"

I took the umbrella. "It was that," I agreed. "Come on. Let's see if I can find a sitting room or parlor. You're my very first visitor and I haven't learned my way around down here yet."

He smiled. "I'll bet you haven't had your morning coffee yet either, have you?"

"You're right . . . would you care to join me?"

He nodded. "Always enjoy a good cup of coffee."

"Well," I assured him, "I do know my way to the kitchen and I do brew a mean cup of coffee. Follow me."

Smiling, he said, "I remember."

As we made our way along the hall, I said, "Thank you for the flowers. It was very thoughtful of you to send them."

"I didn't exactly send them . . . brought them myself, as a matter of fact. I hope you don't mind. I knew the workmen were here and I really wanted to see the inside of this house again." His sigh was just a touch too theatrical. "Sure you don't want to sell . . . ?"

Actually, I thought it pretty presumptuous of him to enter my house while I was away, and yet he had made no attempt to hide his visit. Was it, I wondered, really no more than a desire to see the inside of the house again? Had he, perhaps, been closer to Aunt Sylvia than he had admitted? Or did he have some ulterior motive?

We had reached the kitchen by then, and I turned to face him. For a long moment, we remained silent, both smiling, but also studying each other. Abruptly, harkening back to his earlier question, I asked, "Why are you really here, Mr. Thorne? We both know you don't truly want to buy this place."

For a moment, he looked disconcerted and remained silent.

"Surely you have something more important to do than take care of this mausoleum. Or is there a Mrs. Thorne to cook and clean and sew . . . ?"

Regaining his composure, Thorne shook his head. "No . . . no Mrs. Thorne. You're probably right. I'm not much of a housekeeper." Suddenly he flashed an impish grin. "But maybe I could woo, win, and wed the present owner. Then I'd have both house and housekeeper."

I rolled my eyes heavenward. "You are undoubtedly the last of the great romantics. . . ."

The cat door flapped and Cleo appeared, followed closely by Clarence. Cleo gave Marshall a disdainful glance; Clarence ignored him, went straight to the bowl I had left on the floor the night before. It was empty. Clarence stared at me with expectant eyes, the tip of his tail looped into a question mark above his back, and he rubbed his chin against the edge of the cupboard door.

Marsh leaned forward extending his hand toward Cleo. She gave it a perfunctory sniff, then allowed him to scratch her ears. Marsh began making odd little mewling sounds under his breath and Sheba appeared from nowhere, sat down at his feet, and stared with soft, complacent eyes into his face. He laughed and picked her up, whereupon she burst into noisy song.

I turned from the sink, a can of cat food in my hand, and stared, owl-eyed. Sheba rarely let anyone hold her—even me. Now she nestled against Marshall's chest, golden eyes half-closed, her front paws gently kneading the arm that supported her.

"Amazing!" I said, shaking my head. "Absolutely amazing."

"What's amazing?"

"You . . . Sheba . . . she's not a friendly cat."

"Seems friendly to me." Marsh gave her a hug that elicited a cautionary "Maaou" from Sheba. She twisted her head about and looked up at him. She didn't move again until I had the cat dishes filled and on the floor.

While I busied myself making the coffee, I decided that if Marshall Thorne was good enough for Sheba, he was certainly O.K. with me. Obviously, I was being paranoid thinking there was something sinister about the man. After all, what ulterior motive could he have?

When the pot finished perking, I turned to Marsh once more. "Shall we take our coffee outside?"

"Great idea," he said agreeably. "We'll not have many more mornings like this one."

I gave him a questioning look.

"This your first winter in Washington State?"

I nodded.

"We have lots of gray skies and wet weather up here. It can get pretty cold, too."

"I've noticed how beautiful the fall leaves are. That's something I didn't often see in California."

While we chatted, I put mugs, cream and sugar, and the coffeepot on a large tray. Then Marshall picked it up and followed me to the terrace where, since there was no furniture, we settled ourselves on the steps. The late morning sun was warm, the coffee was strong and hot, and the strait stretched calm and deserted to the horizon. We sat in silence, sipping our coffee, and the throbbing in my temples faded, then disappeared.

"Have you been down to the beach?"

Marsh's voice startled me and I jumped.

"Oh, sorry . . . didn't realize you had wandered so far away."

"Never mind. I guess I'm just a bit tense. I didn't have such a good night last night."

"Trouble?"

"Just an overactive imagination."

His eyes questioned me and I added, "I'm not used to so much quiet. . . ." I sighed, tried to laugh. "It'll be fine once I get the windows draped."

A subtle change in expression clouded his eyes, awakening a germ of unease in me. Then he smiled. "What you need is a great big dog . . . Sylvia always kept a pair of Dobermans after LeBeauforte died. . . ."

"She did? What happened to the dogs after she . . . ?" Oddly, that last word stuck in my throat.

Marsh shrugged. "I don't know."

Suddenly I felt depressed and, well, guilty. I should have asked about pets. Sylvia had given us—me—so much; I could have taken her dogs, done at least that much for her. Besides, I love dogs. I would ask about them next time I saw Stephen, I promised myself.

Marsh stood up. "Come on . . . let's go down to the beach."

"Okay." I, too, rose to my feet. "But let me get the keys first. I don't want to leave the house open." In silence I retrieved my keys and locked the door. When we left the terrace, Clarence and Cleo followed us. However, halfway down the stairs, they disappeared into the undergrowth.

By the time we reached the cove, my legs were

aching with the unaccustomed effort and I was out of breath.

Not so for Marsh. "Come on," he urged. "Let's go take a look at those boulders down at the foot of the cliff. The tide's really a long way out today."

He went striding off down the beach and I broke into a dog trot in a losing effort to keep pace. When I did catch up with him, he was sitting at ease atop a large, damp rock to which starfish and sea urchins clung. His head was tilted back and he was staring at the cliff, his face solemn and thoughtful.

I glanced about looking for a place to sit down, but everything was damp, encrusted with sea moss and festooned with a variety of small mollusks. It was apparent that the area was completely underwater most of the time. Oh, well, I thought, saltwater never ruined a pair of blue jeans and, with a resigned sigh, I eased myself down.

When I had caught my breath, I remarked, "This looks like a great place to swim."

Marshall turned to me, his face solemn. "Don't ever go swimming down here when you're alone. The tides along this coast are treacherous."

"Even here in the cove?"

"Can be. Bad undertow, too . . ." He tilted his head back, stared off into the distance, his face thoughtful. "That's probably what happened to the woman who drowned in town a couple of months ago."

At his words, the sight of Marjory Blake's body, as they pulled it from between the rocks, flashed through my mind. "I was in the parkway when they found her," I whispered. "It was terrible."

Marshall lowered his head, looked at me, a curious expression in his eyes. He said nothing.

"I still find it difficult to believe she just fell off the cliff. . . ."

A spark of interest touched Marshall's face. "Why? What do you think happened to her?"

"I don't know. It just seems odd she would go out there alone and fall over the cliff . . . especially when . . ." I let the sentence trail away. Unaccountably, I didn't want to tell Marshall I had been at the restaurant with Stephen the night it happened.

"When what?" Marshall prompted.

"Oh, nothing, really . . ." But Marshall was staring at me expectantly and I found myself blurting, "Well, you know. She was with that man and surely he didn't just let her go off alone. . . ."

Now Marshall was staring up at the cliff once more, but I thought I detected a tenseness about him.

Why? I wondered. Had Marjory Blake meant something to him?

Marsh pulled a loose shell off the rock and tossed it toward the cliff. "What man?"

"I don't know him. Teddy . . . that's what she called him."

Again he turned his gaze on me. "You saw her that night?"

I was feeling more and more uncomfortable. Something about Marshall Thorne attracted me. I liked him. And yet—suddenly I was again filled with uncertainty. Why did he pretend to want to buy my house? Why was he asking me all these questions?

While these thoughts filled my mind, Marshall

Thorne watched me with questioning eyes. Finally, I laughed, trying to hide my unease, and answered shortly, "Yes, I did." Abruptly, I stood up, dusted the damp sand from my jeans.

Marsh eased himself down from the boulder and glanced at his watch. "Hey . . . it's almost one o'clock . . . I've got to get back to town."

I was puffing again by the time we reached the top of the stairs, and I glanced around while trying to catch my breath. It dawned on me then that Marshall did not have a car. "How did you get out here?" I asked when I could speak.

"Walked . . . there's a path along the top of the cliff."

At his words, I remembered thinking it would not be far along the beach at low tide. Offering him my hand, I smiled. "Thanks again for the flowers."

His fingers closed about mine, held them tight while he said, "Good-bye for now." Then he was gone, striding across the yard and disappearing into the forest.

Impulsively, I turned and walked over to the spot under the trees where I had glimpsed the strange illusion the night before. When a diligent search revealed absolutely nothing, I sighed a little sigh of relief and returned to the house.

The remainder of that day I spent getting acquainted with my new home: learning the floor plan, inspecting room after room, running a cursory inventory of furnishings. It soon became evident that the place was really far too large for me to manage alone, which left me with two choices: take in a roomer, or close part of the house. Probably both, I thought, noting that that gave me a third choice, one that I didn't like any better than I did the first two.

However, later, as I wrote the checks for the work Stephen had supervised for me, I thought how fortunate I was that labor was so cheap here on the island. I could put off making any drastic decisions for a little while. Maybe I could swing it by myself.

As I put my checkbook away and sealed up the last envelope, I congratulated myself on having spent a very satisfying first day in the House on Wiffen Cove. It wasn't until the shadows of the trees spread across the yard, slid up the sides of the house, reached through the windows to fill the rooms with twilight that the uneasiness returned.

Then I hastened to make the rounds of the downstairs, checking the latches on the windows, securing the locks on the doors. And when that was done, I went upstairs and brought down enough sheets to cover the kitchen windows and the glass in the door at the end of the hall.

That door provided access to the backyard, and thence to the garage, which was located in what had originally been the stable and carriage house. It was the one thing about my new home that I did not like.

In fact, I had suggested to Stephen that it would be nice to have an attached garage, or at least one close enough for a breezeway.

"It would be expensive," he had said thoughtfully, then added, "Besides, a garage would detract from the Victorian elegance of the house."

I knew he was right, on both counts. Still, it was a nuisance having to walk so far from the house to the car, and it would be even worse when winter with its foul weather arrived.

Just as I finished hanging the last sheet, Clarence appeared from nowhere and curled himself about my ankles. I scooped him up and he broke into soft, throbbing song. "Just remember . . ." I said to him, "in this world, you can't always have everything just exactly the way you would have it, my friend." Clarence only purred a little louder.

I carried him back to the kitchen where I found the other two sitting beside their empty dishes. Cleo stood up and began to prance, lifting first one paw and then the other, alternately curling and pointing the tips of her toes. I filled their bowls, then fixed a huge salad for myself, and set a fresh pot of coffee to brewing.

When I had finished eating, I filled my cup, grabbed a handful of cookies, and started toward the door thinking to drink my coffee sitting in my little Queen Anne rocker in the back parlor. I had reached the middle of the kitchen when the gentle evening silence was shattered by a wild, high-pitched, demented-banshee wail. Shock halted me in mid-stride. Cup and cookies slipped from my suddenly nerveless fingers. For one endless moment the sound hung crying in the air, then dissolved into silence, leaving me weak and shaken.

The cookies, lying amid the shards of shattered porcelain, turned soggy and brown as they absorbed the still steaming coffee. The cats cowered, Sheba huddled in the Port-a-Pet, her eyes enormous; the other two, under the table, crouched low, their tails thrashing.

When I bent to pick up the pieces of the broken cup, my knees trembled so, I subsided into a kneeling position on the floor. With shaking fingers, I gathered up the larger bits of china and threw them into the trash before sopping up the coffee and sodden cookies with a handful of paper toweling.

I proceeded with care, my movements automatic, and, as much in anger as in grief, I thought about David. Why? Why me? Why did David die and leave me alone? And as quickly as I thought the thoughts, came the answer: it's your fault David is dead. . . .

"No!" the word burst from me. Then I said more softly, "No, no, no." I was crying, the tears salty on my lips, and when Cleo thrust her round silky head under my elbow to rest upon my knee, I sat down on the floor, gathered her into my arms, and buried my face in her soft warm fur.

It isn't fair! I kept thinking. All those years after the accident—even in the beginning when the nightmares were so bad, I never fell apart. No matter how miserable I felt inside, how frightened of what the future might bring, I maintained a brave front. I smiled when my heart was breaking, and I kept going when I was so tired and discouraged, all I wanted to do was die.

Now that's behind me. This house is supposed to be my refuge, my new beginning. Instead, the damned place is full of noises I can't explain; the cats are *seeing things*; and my nerves are shot!

I don't know how long I sat with those ideas squirreling round in my head; but my final thought was, Well, I won't let it scare me away. This is my house, and I'm going to live in it!

With that, I put Cleo down and stood up. I got another paper towel, dried my eyes and blew my nose, then squatted down and cleaned up the rest of the mess on the kitchen floor.

And when everything was tidy, I took a deep breath, moved out into the hall, and stood staring at the rear door. What's out there? I wondered. I felt certain the sound I had just heard was the same sound I had heard that first evening I came to Wiffen Cove. If only I had asked Stephen.

Still, as long as I stayed inside, I would be safe— and this close to town—it couldn't be anything very dangerous. After all, what could it be but some kind of animal? What else would make such a terrifying sound? I shivered.

Something brushed against my leg and a startled gasp escaped my lips, but it was only Sheba, come out into the hall seeking reassurance. I picked her up and laid my cheek against the top of her sleek head. Dear old Sheba—she had always been David's favorite. She had spent hours curled up on his knees in the wheelchair. I moved slowly toward the stairway, one arm supporting Sheba, the other hand scratching gently behind her ears, my mind busy with memories—bittersweet memories.

We were halfway up the stairs when Sheba suddenly stiffened in my grasp and began to rumble deep in her throat. Then, before I could gather my wits about me, she dug her claws deep into my shoulder and launched herself in a mighty leap over the banister to land in the hallway below. There she crouched, ears back, sputtering and hissing while she stared with baleful eyes at the emptiness above me at the top of the stairs.

# NINE

Silence. Total, complete. Sheba had ceased her imprecations; indeed, all three cats had disappeared. Seemingly of its own volition, my head jerked round and my unwilling gaze sought the top of the stairs. The hallway above was full of shadow. Nothing more. At least nothing I could see. I listened, straining to hear some telltale sound, but the thudding of my own heart was too loud in my ears.

And still I stood, afraid to go up, afraid to go back. If only I could reach the phone. If only there were some way to get to my car without having to cross that unprotected expanse of yard. Dear God! I thought, I am so alone. . . .

I might have remained there, crouched against the wall until morning, had not a sudden muffled crash from somewhere in the midst of the house sent me bolting up the stairs and into my room where I slammed and locked the door behind me, and switched on the lights. In their soft glow, the bedroom looked snug and welcoming; but the blackness of night huddled just outside the undraped window and I wondered what demons might be crouching there, peering in at me. It was such a ridiculous thought, it brought my rampaging imagination up short.

You've got to stop letting every little thing upset you, I told myself. So those cats have been doing some peculiar things! Don't they always? And letting noises in the night send you into a panic! You'd scarcely notice them if the sun was shining.

It was a good lecture, and I did begin to settle down. Nevertheless, I grabbed up my nightgown and retired to the bathroom to change. When I pulled off my T-shirt, I could see smears of dried blood on my shoulder where Sheba's claws had dug deep. I couldn't help thinking that Sheba had never before drawn blood, but I refused to let my imagination take over from there.

I stepped into the shower and turned it on, and immediately turned it off again. The hiss and rattle of the water, drowning out the silence, perhaps masking some other sound, was too much for my frayed nerves. In the end, I sponged the blood from my shoulder with my washcloth.

By the time I was dry once more and in my nightdress, I had regained my composure. Still, I thought, it would be foolhardy not to exercise caution. So I leaned my ear against the door, straining for any sound from the bedroom. All was silent. I took a deep breath and warily cracked the door. With one eye pressed to the opening, I peered about. The room was empty.

Of course, it's empty, I told myself. You, Kimberly D'Ahl, are letting your imagination run away with you. Now, just open the door and go to bed. Stop acting like a fool! Thus berating myself, I at last worked up enough courage to leave the bathroom.

Crossing quickly to the bed, I paused only long enough to switch on the bedside lamp, then slipped, with a sigh of relief, under the covers.

Not until my head was on the pillow did I realize the overhead light was still on. I swore softly, got out of bed once more, crossed the room, and switched it off. As I turned from the wall and started back toward my bed, the bedside lamp winked out, leaving me in total darkness. I spun around, flipped the wall switch on once more, but the room remained dark.

Don't panic now! I warned myself as I turned back toward the center of the room and stood, straining my eyes against the gloom, seeking some point of reference. But clouds had overshadowed the moon filling my room with an impenetrable stygian darkness. And then, from somewhere came a faint but unmistakable swoosh of sound. A cold, musty breath of air stirred the blackness around me, crawled over my bare arms and shoulders, touched my lips, and filled my nostrils with the odor of dust and decay.

Before I had time to react, something struck my arm, the impact hard enough to stagger me. I tripped, fell to one knee, struggled back to my feet, and tried to see what was in the room with me but I could not. I tried to call out, but strangely no sound would form in my throat. My legs refused to hold me longer, and as consciousness slipped from me, I slid down, down, down. . . .

I awoke in the morning to find myself lying in my bed. The sun, spilling its shining rays through the alcove window, filled my room with glorious golden light. I lay quite still on my back, breathing slowly and deeply. My mouth was dry, my head ached, I felt groggy. I glanced at the clock. It was after ten! I couldn't remember when I had last slept this late. Perhaps, I thought, I'm coming down with the flu.

Sidetracked by that idea, it took me a moment to remember where I was. Then, faster than I could sort them out, events of the previous night flooded my mind: the darkness, the fear, the sound—but how had I gotten back to bed?

Despite my queasy stomach, I forced myself to sit up and look about the room. As far as I could tell, everything was as it should be: the door was closed, the key still in the lock; my robe lay across the foot of the bed. Then, I reached out and flipped the switch on my bedside lamp. Instantly, the bulb glowed with light.

But that couldn't be! Or could I have imagined the whole episode? or dreamed it? I had had nightmares for months after the accident. Night after night I had wakened in a cold sweat, trembling with fear, yet never able to clearly remember what had so terrified me. But surely, I thought, that can't be happening again; I won't let it happen again!

I slipped out of bed, shrugged off my nightgown, and padded barefoot across the room to the bath. A quick shower is what I need, I told myself, and I turned on the water to let it run hot while I brushed my hair. I glanced in the mirror, then stopped, staring in disbelief at my reflection. On one shoulder, the claw marks left by Sheba were clearly visible, an angry red against the white of my flesh. But it was not the sight of the wounds left by Sheba's claws that set my heart to pounding, my brain to racing; it was a huge purple bruise on my arm.

My breath caught in my throat and I leaned nearer the mirror, disbelieving. Only then did I perceive the broad smear of dust across my cheek.

Instinctively, I whirled about, turning my back on the mirror, as if by refusing to look I could make the nightmare marks on my flesh go away. Teeth clenched against the hysteria rising in my throat, I reached automatically for the door, closed and locked it, then stepped into the steaming shower, my thoughts in chaos. I stood unmoving as the needles of spray beat against me, let the heat of the water coursing over me soothe the temptation to panic.

Not until I had regained a semblance of calm did I try to recall exactly what had happened the night before; but I could remember nothing except the terror and the final plunge into oblivion. Did I just faint? I asked myself. Bruise my arm against something as I fell? But if I was unconscious, how did I get into bed? And how in the world did I get that smear of dust on my face? It made no sense!

And then I began to laugh. You are being very silly, I told myself. Obviously I had had a nightmare. It had sparked my imagination. What I had seen in the mirror was no smear of dirt on my face, it was an illusion—a flaw in the mirror, perhaps. Of course, that was it.

I turned off the shower and again confronted my image in the glass. There was no flaw in the mirror; but the illusion was gone; no dirty smear. I shrugged. Probably it had been a shadow. But the bruise on my arm had not disappeared. . . .

A moment longer I gazed at that purple blotch, then turned away. It's nothing, I told myself, nothing. I bumped into something in the dark. I did wake up, safe and sound in my bed, didn't I? If someone had wanted to do me harm, why didn't they?

Continuing to reassure myself, I returned to the bedroom. Once there, however, I was sorely tempted to flop down on the bed and pull the covers over my head, which was still throbbing. And my mouth was dry, tacky, even after my teeth had been brushed. What I really need, I decided, is a cup of coffee.

I pulled on a pair of blue jeans and shrugged into a T-shirt emblazoned with a stalking leopardess. Then I stumbled my way down the stairs. The three cats were sitting patiently at the bottom, staring up at me with hopeful eyes. Clarence got to his feet and twined himself about my ankle. I leaned down, picked him up, snuggled him against my shoulder as I made my way across the dining room, through the service hall, and into the kitchen.

I stopped just inside the door and looked around. Somehow, something was different. An uneasy prickling sensation crawled across my scalp. I stared about trying to discover what was amiss but I couldn't put my finger on it. I sighed. Damn, I thought, I am really letting my imagination run away with me.

Making a determined effort to ignore my fears of the night past, I fed the cats, put the coffee on to perk, then sat down at the kitchen table to plan my day. I have too much time on my hands. That's why my imagination is playing tricks on me. As soon as

I've had my coffee, I thought, I'll go into town. I'll check with Stephen again about finding a roomer. Perhaps just having someone else in the house will help.

I was getting up to pour myself a cup of coffee when the doorbell chimed. It was Stephen, and the very sight of him sent a surge of relief flowing through me. "Oh, Stephen," I said, "I'm so glad to see you!" and impulsively I threw my arms about him, hugged him tight.

He rubbed his cheek against the top of my head. "This is the kind of greeting I like," he murmured.

I stepped away and smiled up at him. "Come on back to the kitchen. I just made a pot of coffee."

"I can't stay . . . only stopped by to make sure you were all right."

"I'm fine," I lied.

"I tried to call you. When I didn't get an answer, I was worried."

"You called this morning?"

He glanced at his watch. "A little after nine . . ."

"That's strange. The phone usually wakes me."

"It's not important." His smile as he spoke was lazy and intimate. "I'm glad you're all right."

The relief I had felt at first sight of him was replaced by a sudden intense physical awareness. I turned quickly away and started up the hall.

Despite his statement that he couldn't stay, he followed me back to the kitchen and sat down at the table. I poured us each a cup of coffee, then sat down opposite him. Clarence jumped onto my knees and burst into song. I leaned forward and rubbed my cheek against his silky ears.

When I looked at Stephen again, he was sipping

his coffee, his eyes contemplating me over the rim of his cup. He put the cup down. "How are you getting along?"

I sighed. Now that someone was with me, my fears of the night past seemed vague and a bit silly. Finally I said, "Oh, all right."

Stephen lifted his brows in a questioning glance. "Are you sure you're all right? You don't sound your usual bright little self."

I tried to smile reassuringly. "Oh, I tend to let my imagination work overtime."

"And what have you been imagining?"

"Well, now don't laugh. It's just that the cats aren't settling in the way they should—absolutely refuse to go upstairs, and I keep hearing a weird sound."

"Don't tell me you think the place is haunted. . . ."

"Of course not!" I was angered and hurt by his flip remark.

Stephen knew it. He was quick to apologize. "I'm sorry. I know it can be a little scary in a big old place like this, especially when you're alone. So tell me, what do you mean . . . _weird_ sound?"

I thought for a moment trying to find words to describe it. "Like something shrieking, I guess."

Solemnly, Stephen's eyes studied my face, but I had the impression he was suppressing a smile. "What do you think this something might be?"

"I don't know," I snapped, feeling defensive. "That's why I'm asking you."

He shook his head. "From your description . . . could be any number of things . . . the wind, or an animal . . . could it have been a dog howling at the moon?"

Dog! Once again I had almost forgotten. "Could it be Sylvia's dogs? What happened to the poor things?"

"Ha! Poor things, nothing! Those two are living in the lap of luxury being cared for by their very own vet."

For an instant, something about Stephen's reply niggled, but I brushed it aside. "Well, then . . ." I shrugged. "I don't know. . . ." I took a deep breath before adding, all in a rush, "You don't think it could be anything dangerous?"

Now Stephen did laugh. "Absolutely not. There's nothing on the island that's dangerous . . . unless maybe some of the tourists we get."

"I suppose you're right," I agreed reluctantly. "I guess I just have too much time on my hands. I need to get some sort of project started. I've never lived like this before . . . no demands on my time . . . no responsibilities."

"I thought that was one of the main reasons for moving into the house, to rid yourself of all responsibilities."

"What made you think that?" Somehow the remark annoyed me.

"That's what everyone wants—no responsibility. Just plenty of money and time to do what they please."

"I don't believe that!" The words came out a bit more sharply than I intended and I added, "I think most people just want the freedom to accept those responsibilities they feel best equipped to handle."

Stephen smiled at me. "Do you know your eyes change color when you're angry?"

"I'm not angry!"

"Good," Stephen nodded, but he was still smiling at me as if I were a small child. Then he sighed and his face sobered. "Look, I've got to be out of town for a few days on business, but plan on having dinner with me on Friday. We'll go someplace special and dance."

He had risen to his feet as he spoke, and I walked with him to the front door. He paused in the muted light of the entryway and looked down at me. Again that rush of tingling warmth flowed through me, and I would have looked away had he not hooked a finger under my chin. For a long moment he studied my face. Then he bent his head and his lips brushed mine. "How sweet you are," he whispered, then he opened the door and strode down the steps to the path.

I watched until he rounded the corner of the house, but he didn't look back. I was both surprised and tormented by the physical sensations his touch has wakened. Am I falling in love with Stephen? I wondered. Was it possible, I wondered, to want a man and not love him? I certainly didn't feel about Stephen the way I had about David. . . .

And thinking of David, Marshall Thorne popped into my mind. Don't be so silly! I told myself, and marched back up the hall. In the kitchen once more, I poured myself another cup of coffee and sat down. Clarence jumped onto my lap again, and offered his chin for scratching. I laughed—Clarence had a talent for making me laugh. I pushed all the romantic nonsense out of my head and returned to my earlier thoughts.

With Stephen out of town, I'd have to ask Vera about a roomer. What a depressing development. On the other hand, she would probably know more about finding someone than Stephen.

Suiting actions to thought, I ran upstairs, changed my clothes, and was on the way to town before I could change my mind. I drove directly to the office of Enders and Enders and parked. I didn't notice the CLOSED sign in the window until I tried to open the door. I glanced at my watch. It was only eleven o'clock—much too early for Vera to have gone to lunch. How strange, I thought, especially with Stephen out of town. I stood on the sidewalk for a few minutes hoping she would suddenly appear. That proved futile, so I got back into the car and drove over to the post office to pick up my mail.

There was a notice from the company that was readying the new window coverings. I was relieved to read that they had everything ready to deliver and hoped to meet with me before the end of the week. There was also a letter from Moss and Moss that stated they had had an offer on some of the things they were holding on consignment and wanted me to get in touch with them.

As I was leaving the post office, the same young woman who had spoken to me the day I painted the picture of the Tor started up the steps toward me. Our eyes met and she smiled. "Hello," she called. "How did the painting turn out?"

I shrugged and tried to assume a crestfallen expression. "I never finished it," I admitted, then laughed. "It really wasn't all that good."

"But it was better than most," she replied, repeating what she had said the day we first met.

I thanked her and started to move down the steps, but she put out her hand and stopped me. For a moment she didn't speak, but glanced around with a quick nervous movement of her head. When she turned back, she regarded me intently. "Are you really living out there in that House on Wiffen Cove?" Her voice was so low I could just hear the words.

Mystified by her actions, I only nodded.

Again she swiveled her head and looked about. Then she turned back to me. "Aren't you afraid out there . . . all alone?"

I gazed at her in astonishment. How, I wondered, did she know I was all alone, and why should she care? Finally, I shook my head, no, and added, "Should I be?"

"Well, I wouldn't spend a night out there even if you promised me the whole . . ." Her voice had risen and she broke off suddenly, hesitated, then finished rather lamely, "No matter what you paid me."

"Why not?" Although her remark sounded like dialogue from a third-rate whodunit, I felt my nerves tighten.

Again her eyes searched my face before she spoke. "After what happened to Ms. Belgedes?" She shrugged and looked away.

I shivered. Mama would have said someone was walking over my grave. "Why? What did happen to her?"

"You don't know?" The girl's expression emphasized her amazement at my lack of knowledge.

"Only that she died. . . ." As I said the words, I felt a surge of shame, shame that I had cared so little about Aunt Sylvia that I had never even inquired as to the cause of her death, and I wondered how I could have been so callous.

But the girl was speaking again: "The police said it was an accident, but none of us believe that. We think she was murdered!"

I could only stare at the woman. Murdered! I shook my head in disbelief. Then I blurted, "What do you mean?"

Again the girl glanced about before replying. "It was no accident that killed Sylvia Belgedes. It wasn't suicide, either, as some of the people around here would like to think. Ms. Belgedes would never have killed herself . . . not like that anyway. Someone got in that big old house . . . it wouldn't be hard to do . . . and murdered her."

"How . . . how . . . ?" I couldn't bring myself to say the words, but the girl understood my question.

"They say she took an overdose of sleeping pills or something. They think she must have gone to bed, then changed her mind because they found her lying at the bottom of the stairs. It was the fall that killed her. It broke her neck. But what was so strange . . . they say she had dust and cobwebs all over her and a big purple bruise on her arm. . . ."

"But couldn't that have happened when she fell?"

"Not if she died in the fall. . . ."

# TEN

Before leaving town, I called the drapers and arranged to have the window coverings installed the next Monday. I also talked to Claire Moss. The offer she described seemed reasonable, and we easily reached an agreement. Then I went to Mom's Café and lingered over a piece of pie and coffee. I even went to the grocery store and picked up some potato chips and cookies I didn't need. Last of all, I returned to Enders and Enders, but the CLOSED sign was still in the window. I could think of nothing else to keep me in town, so, under a sky that had turned a uniform leaden gray from horizon to horizon, I drove slowly back to Wiffen Cove fighting a mounting sense of dread.

It was the dread of returning to that house with its warren of shadow-filled rooms and drafty, echoing halls that had kept me dawdling about town, all the while assuring myself that the girl's story concerning Aunt Sylvia's death had been more hearsay than fact.

It was close to five o'clock when I left the protection of the trees and drove over the crest of the hill above Wiffen Cove. A stiff wind, blowing in across the strait, lashed my car and splattered the windshield with the first monstrous drops from a fast-approaching rainstorm. At the same instant, I noticed a bright red MG parked under the porte cochere and I felt a surge of relief. It didn't matter to whom the car might belong. It meant that for a little while, at least, I would not have to face the house alone.

As I approached, the door of the small vehicle opened and Marshall Thorne got out. I edged my car in beside his and he walked around to open the door for me.

"Hi," he said, offering a helpful hand. "I hope you don't mind my dropping in on you like this. I couldn't find you in the phone book."

I wondered why he didn't call information, then dismissed the thought. I felt a quite genuine rush of pleasure at the sight of him and I smiled in greeting. "It's good to see you," I said. "I'm glad you didn't wait to call first . . . especially since I wasn't here to answer the phone."

"Maybe you'll give me the number before I leave."

I nodded assent. "Have you been waiting long?"

"Didn't seem long. I wandered around out in the garden . . . you've done wonders out there, and the view is always new."

As we talked, he got my bag of groceries from the backseat and we climbed the steps to the ironbound double doors. Stephen had given me a dozen keys, more or less, the day I moved into the house. They had been left with him by the lawyer. I still had not discovered which keys opened which doors, but I did know that the huge brass one adorned with a lion's head grip opened the porte cochere entrance.

I turned the key in the lock, pushed the doors wide, and we both stepped inside.

"This way," I said, and Marshall followed me through the narrow back hall to the dining room and hence to the kitchen. He set the bag of groceries on the counter, then picked up Sheba, who lolled back against his arm and gazed with adoring golden eyes into his face.

"What is it with you and that cat?" I asked, still amazed that Sheba would let him hold her.

"She's a very wise old lady," he chuckled. "She knows who her friends are."

"Sure you don't have a catnip mouse in your pocket?"

Marshall assumed an aggrieved air. "That's not a very flattering attitude. Hasn't it occurred to you that I'm just an especially nice guy!"

I laughed. "You're right," I admitted. "Who am I to disagree with Sheba."

I glanced at my watch. It was after five o'clock, and I suddenly felt the urge to do something special. "How about some tea?"

Marshall smiled. "I'd enjoy that, thanks."

He sat down at the kitchen table and we chatted easily while I put the groceries away. Then I brought out an elegant tea service of heavy antique silver that I had found among Sylvia's effects, and prepared the tea.

When everything was ready, I gave Marsh the tray and sent him off to the sitting room where the windows overlooked the strait—the one with the oak paneling and built-in bookcases. He said he knew the one I meant, that he had spent many an hour there with Sylvia learning to play chess.

I ran upstairs, washed my face, and changed into a pair of pale ivory cotton knit pants and an oversized matching top. Then I ran a comb through my hair and redid my lipstick.

Downstairs once more, I entered the sitting room to find Marshall hunkered down in front of the fireplace staring into the flames that leaped and crackled there. At the sound of my footsteps, he rose, turning, all in one fluid movement, to face me.

I continued around the table to stand beside him, hands outstretched to the warmth. "Oh, I'm glad you thought of the fire."

His smile widened and he said almost shyly, "Sylvia always liked a fire. On days like this, we'd toss on a couple of logs and then sit over there"—he nodded toward the drum table in the bow window—"and play chess. . . ."

Outside, the rain was falling steadily now, lashed by an ugly wind that whipped the trees and moaned under the eaves and about the corners of the house. We moved back around the oak table and settled ourselves on the settee facing the fireplace.

I pulled the tea tray nearer, poured, and handed a cup to Marsh, then watched, aghast, as he added four lumps of sugar and a splash of milk. I shook my head and poured a cup for myself. Then we leaned back companionably, and watched the yellow and orange flames dancing over the coals on the hearth.

The rich, full-bodied aroma of the tea; the rattle of the rain on the windowpane behind us; the warmth radiating from the fire, all combined to ease the tension I had been striving to hide from Marshall. We sat in silence for a while, then I turned to him and said, "Tell me about Sylvia."

Marshall leaned forward and put his cup on the tray. "What would you like to know?"

"Everything you can remember. Describe her first."

"Well, she was pretty . . . tall, slim, dark blue eyes . . . her hair was dark, too." He smiled, his expression warm with nostalgia. "I think I told you she was my first love. She was beautiful."

"The older woman syndrome?"

"Might have been . . . but even after I got over the puppy love, I found her a very attractive woman . . . bright, strong-willed."

He picked up a cheese-laden cracker, popped it into his mouth.

I refilled his cup, handed it to him.

Accepting it, he grinned reminiscently. "I really didn't like tea when I was a kid, but I was always afraid to say no to Sylvia. I just heaped in the sugar and drank it!"

I laughed. "Is that what you're doing today?"

He shot me a sidelong glance, his face coloring slightly. "Oh no. I've learned to really enjoy a good cup of tea."

I fixed him with a questioning stare. "Really?"

"All right! So I'm not crazy about tea." He paused, gave me that impish grin. "But the company is terrific."

I had to laugh, and when our eyes met, an unexpected and altogether unsettling awareness flowed between us. He leaned toward me and I thought for a moment he was going to kiss me, it seemed so natural. Instead, he got to his feet and put another log on the fire.

I stared at his back in confusion, but by the time

he resumed his place beside me on the settee I had regained my composure and I said, "So tell me more about Aunt Sylvia."

He stared moodily into the fire for a while before continuing. "After I got to know her, she laughed a lot. She would ask me questions about people in the town. . . ."

"Did she have lots of friends?"

He gave me an odd look: questioning, assessing, maybe both, before continuing. "About friends, I'm not sure; but she seemed to know a lot of the townspeople even though she apparently never left this house except to walk in the garden or go down to the cove." His face took on a tentative, withdrawn expression.

"Your visits must have meant a lot to her."

"Maybe . . . I hope so. Anyway, she would ask me about this one and that one, and she always seemed to find my answers amusing. I don't know why . . . maybe she just wanted an excuse to laugh. I think she was a very lonely woman. I didn't realize it at the time, of course, but now . . ."

He sighed and fell silent; I couldn't read the expression in his eyes. The silence grew and I prompted, "How old were you then? How old do you think she was?"

He took a deep breath, stretched his shoulders. "I was maybe eight or nine the first time I knocked on the door. After that I used to see her off and on until I left for the university." He frowned, his brows drawing together in the effort to recall. "I don't have any idea how old she was. The last time I saw her, she was probably in her thirties . . . thirty-five maybe. She never seemed to change. . . ."

Something jogged somewhere in the back of my mind, and then I remembered. "Stephen Enders told me that he and Sylvia were friends . . . sort of. . . ."

Marshall turned and looked at me, shrugged. "I don't know. She never mentioned him and I never saw him here. Have you known him long?"

Unaccountably, I blushed, but I answered calmly enough. "Not really. His firm was given the job of caretaking the place until David . . . until I made up my mind about moving up here. Mr. Enders has been very helpful."

I was certain Marshall had not missed my reaction to his question, but he said nothing and I added, "Do you know him?"

"Not really . . . I know of him. . . ."

"Did you know LeBeauforte?"

"I saw him a couple of times, but I never met him. Sylvia never said, but I always knew it would be better if I didn't stay when he was home."

"That seems odd. Maybe you just imagined it."

He rubbed his nose with the knuckles of his left hand. "Well, maybe . . . but I don't think so."

"Then why do you think she didn't want you here when LeBeauforte was home?"

"I have no idea," he said solemnly. "I wish I did."

At that moment, a horrendous clap of thunder followed almost immediately by a flash of brilliant, blue-white light ripped through the room, followed by another tremendous crash and roll of thunder, and almost simultaneously another blaze of lightning lit the night. The deafening barrage, punctuated by blinding flashes of light seemed to go on and on.

As suddenly as it had begun, the sound faded, and I realized we were both on our feet. I was cowering in Marsh's arms, my hands gripped tight on the lapels of his jacket, my cheek pressed against its rough tweed. The room was dark save for the glow from the hearth.

I was trembling uncontrollably yet I had never before been frightened by thunder and lightning. In fact, I had always enjoyed the wild beauty, the unbridled power of an electrical storm. I could only assume it was some indication of the tension that had been building inside me ever since I took up residence in the House on Wiffen Cove. Marsh continued to hold me, one hand gently patting me between the shoulder blades just as my mother had done when I was a little girl, frightened by some now long forgotten terror that went bump in the night. "It's all right . . ." Marsh kept murmuring, "it's all right."

And while he held me, the tension drained away to be replaced by a feeling of utter contentment. It started somewhere deep inside, growing and spreading, filling my whole being with quiet happiness. I wanted him to go on holding me like that forever.

Dreamily, I lifted my face to his. The world slipped into slow motion and we stared at each other for one interminable moment. I could almost feel his lips on mine, but instead of kissing me, he gripped my shoulders with his hands and gently moved us apart. Then he turned and walked over to stand before the window gazing out into the night.

I stood very still, unable to think. Too many emotions had been stirred. I found I wasn't able to sort out in my own mind just what had happened.

The light from the fire flickered. Marshall began fumbling around in the drawer of the drum table. "Sylvia used to keep extra candles in here . . . yes, here we are."

I heard the scratch of a match, then a soft wavering light filled the room and the world began to move at its normal pace once more.

"Now all we need is a candle holder." Marsh's voice was calm.

"Here," I said, handing him a saucer. "Use this."

"Thanks." He tipped the candle, dripped some wax into its bottom to anchor the candle.

"What happened to the lights?"

"Lightning . . . wind　maybe . . . must　have damaged a pole."

I was surprised at how matter-of-fact our voices sounded.

"Do you have any oil lamps?"

"Lamps?" I had seen some someplace. Then I remembered. "There are a couple in the pantry. . . ."

Cupping the guttering flame of the candle in his palm, Marshall followed me out into the hall. My shadow preceded us, wavering and undulating toward the darker shadows ahead. In the kitchen, Marshall helped me locate the lamps. There were two, each still half full of oil. Marsh removed the chimneys, deftly trimmed the wicks, and set the lamps burning as if it were an everyday occurrence.

The cats appeared, melting out of the shadows under the table, their eyes pools of liquid fire in the lamplight. I looked at my watch. It was close to seven o'clock.

"Poor babies," I said, and I suddenly felt like crying. "I usually feed them at six."

"I think they'll survive," Marshall soothed. "They don't look underfed."

I found a can of cat food and pushed it into the opener. Nothing happened. "Damn!" I exploded, and whacked it with the can.

Marsh's voice, calm and soothing, interrupted me. "Easy, there. That thing's not going to work till the power's back on. . . ."

I put the can down and turned to face him. "How long do you think that will be?" My voice was tight.

He was half sitting on the edge of the table holding Sheba, but he was watching me. "Could be a few minutes . . . could be a few days."

I stared at him while the tension built across my shoulders, up the back of my neck. He must be joking, I thought. Aloud I said, "A few days . . . what do you mean?"

"Sometimes it takes them a while to get all the lines back up. You could be without power for several days."

I was trembling again and the tension had become a dull throbbing in my temples. "But I can't be without power. . . ." The minute the words were said, I realized how childish I sounded.

"You'll be all right," Marsh said soothingly. "You have candles and lamps, and enough firewood for tonight, at least."

"But several days . . . I never thought . . ."

"You do know our winters can be quite severe . . . ?"

I just gaped at him.

"There is a furnace in this place?"

"A furnace?" I looked about helplessly, suddenly aware that the kitchen was like an icebox. "I think . . . there must be . . . oh, I don't know!" My voice broke and a violent shiver ran down my back.

"Hey." Marsh reached out a calming hand, laid it gently on my arm. His fingers were warm against my icy flesh. "Why, you're cold as ice." He put Sheba on the floor and took off his jacket. "Come on, let's go back to the parlor and I'll build up the fire." As he spoke he was wrapping his jacket about me and steering me toward the kitchen door.

Abruptly, I balked. "No. Not yet. The cats need their dinner. I've got an old-fashioned can opener in the drawer."

Marsh grinned. "Let me do the honors," he said, pushing me toward the door. "You go back and stand close to the fireplace. I'll be along soon as the cats are fed."

I hesitated, but Marsh said, "Go!"

Back in the parlor once more, I set the lamp I was carrying on the mantel, and turned to stand with my back to the fire. The storm had passed. Silence, accentuated by the settling and creaking of the old house, pressed in on me. The minutes crept by. I picked up the poker, stirred the fire. What can be taking Marsh so long? I wondered.

When at last I heard the soft thud of his returning footsteps, a long sigh of relief escaped my lips. Then he was at the door and I waited expectantly; but he didn't enter. So I called, "Just a minute," put down the poker, and hurried across the room to let him in.

But when I opened the door, the hallway before

me was filled with blackness. "Marsh?" The word was only a whisper. "Marsh, answer me. . . ."

No answer came, but something brushed against my leg. Startled, I skittered sideways, tripped over a throw rug, and fell sprawling to the floor.

At that moment, the doorway filled with lamplight to be followed shortly by Marsh. I raised my head, shook it, rolled over, and sat up. Marsh set his lamp on the table, then reached down and helped me to my feet.

"What were you doing down . . ." he began, but the expression on my face stopped him in mid-sentence. "What's the matter?"

I gazed at him in silence, trying to understand what had happened. Finally, I said, "I heard you . . . in the hall . . . but you weren't there."

"I'm here," he answered cautiously.

"I opened the door and you weren't there . . . and then something touched me. . . ."

"Must have been Clarence. See, there he is over by the fireplace."

I turned my head to look at Clarence sitting non-chalantly before the dying embers of the fire, his eyes reflecting their orange glow. Then I turned back to stare at Marshall.

"But I heard you . . . your footsteps in the hall . . ." There was uncertainty in my voice.

"Sound carries in these old houses. I'm sorry if you were frightened. Come on. Put this blanket around you. I ran upstairs and got it since you were so cold. Now sit down while I build up the fire." As he spoke, Marsh bundled me into a down comforter, then settled me gently but firmly into a corner of the sofa.

My eyes followed him as he went about the task of replenishing the fire, but my mind was full of turmoil. All of the things that had happened were whirling about in my head: the noises, the way the cats behaved, that note with its implied warning, Marjory Blake lying dead amid the rocks and seaweed, and that girl saying Sylvia had been murdered. . . .

Marsh gave the fire one more poke. "There, that'll do it. This room, at least, will be warm again in no time." He returned to the sofa and sat down beside me. "And how are you? Feeling better now?"

I nodded, managed what I hoped was a smile. "I know I've been behaving rather badly. I'm sorry."

He scrutinized my face. "Are you sure you're all right?"

"Of course." I tried to sound unconcerned. "Just a case of nerves . . . and a very creative imagination."

Still he stood, looking at me. Finally he said, "Don't be too hard on yourself. It's understandable, you know, being upset. After the stress and strain of your husband's illness, then losing him. It's not unusual when something like that is all over to find that you're overwrought." He paused, smiled apologetically, then added, "My boss keeps a sign on his desk that says, 'When this is over, I'm going to have a nervous breakdown. I deserve it.'"

I was afraid the smile I gave him was halfhearted, but I said, "Thanks, I needed that."

He continued to study my face, but didn't offer any comment. Then he glanced at his watch. "Hey! It's nearly eight o'clock. I'd better be on my way."

My heart contracted and I thought, I'll be all

alone again. I wanted to shout, "No, don't go, please don't go!" but I forced myself to say, "I'm so glad you stopped by." We both stood up. I wriggled out of the comforter, slipped off his jacket, and handed it to him. "Thank you," I said.

He thrust his arms into the sleeves, and shrugged the garment up over his shoulders.

"I'm sorry I let myself be frightened by the storm. I'm usually not such a coward. I . . ." There seemed nothing else to say. Lamely I added, "Thanks for all your help."

"My pleasure," he said. "Always glad to help a fair maiden in distress." We both laughed, but his face sobered immediately. "Don't bother to see me out," he said. "Stay here and keep warm. The cold weather seems to have come early this year."

I walked with him to the parlor door. He opened it a crack, then turned back to me. "Thanks for the tea." The impish smile was in evidence again. "It was better than Sylvia used to make."

Then he was gone and I moved slowly back to the sofa. The silence closed in again. A log on the hearth snapped, throwing up a shower of sparks, the clock in its glass dome chimed the hour: eight-thirty. Clarence jumped up beside me and climbed into my lap. I wondered idly where Sheba and Cleo might be, if the cold weather had settled in to stay, when Emma and Jerry might come for a visit. It was like mentally walking on eggshells, keeping my thoughts away from the fear lurking so close to the surface of my mind.

And then the footsteps came again, padding swiftly up the hall. My heart began to pound, my throat constricted painfully. The footsteps stopped, there came a rapping on the door. My breath froze, my heart missed a beat. Who or what was out there?

So great was my fear, I scarcely recognized his voice when Marsh called cheerily, "Sorry, Kim, I'm back already." He pushed the door open as he spoke and started toward me. "I've got a flat tire." Abruptly, he stopped. "Oh, lord! I am so sorry! Did I frighten you again?"

He crossed quickly to the sofa and sank down beside me, took my trembling hands in his. "Something's the matter," he said, more to himself than to me. "You shouldn't be this terrified by a bit of lightning . . . a few footsteps in the hall. Tell me, Kim, what's wrong? Why are you so frightened?"

I opened my mouth to speak, but even as the words formed in my mind, I could hear how paranoid they would sound: strange noises? flighty cats? a bruise on my arm? What nonsense! Stephen had said it was nonsense.

And then I heard my voice asking, "What happened to Aunt Sylvia, Marsh. How did she die?"

He shook his head from side to side. "So that's it. Someone just had to tell you all the rumors."

I nodded. "Some girl I don't even know . . . she said Sylvia was murdered . . . right here in this house. . . ."

Marsh was looking intently into my face, and now he nodded. "There was some speculation . . . gossip . . . but the police confirmed that it was an accident. Shame somebody didn't clear all that up for you right away. No wonder you're frightened."

He clasped both of my hands in one of his before covering them with the other, and we sat silent for a few moments. Then, without quite knowing how it happened, I found myself telling him everything, in detail, about the things that had been happening and the awful feeling that I was not alone in that great warren of a house.

He listened without speaking, nodding his head from time to time. His eyes never left my face. And when I had at last told him everything, he still sat silent, his face bemused.

Then he sighed, reached out and patted my shoulder, murmured, "That's quite a story. . . ." He stared moodily into the fireplace, then got up and put another log on the glowing embers.

When he returned to the sofa and had settled himself once more, he asked, his expression thoughtful, "Do I remember rightly . . . you did say Sylvia was your husband's aunt?"

"Um humm . . . his father's sister."

"Did she visit often?"

"David and me? No. I never met her."

"But your husband . . . he knew her?"

"Not really. He said he only saw her once when he was about twelve. He didn't even remember her very well, but . . ."

Just then the clock on the mantel began to chime, and I glanced at it. It surprised me to see that it was nine o'clock, and I remembered at the same moment that we had not yet had dinner.

"Look at the time! Are you hungry?"

For a moment, I thought Marsh was about to say something else, then he glanced at his watch as if to corroborate the time before replying, "Now that you mention it, I'm famished!"

"Then do let me fix you something—to make up

for my silly behavior and what I've put you through. I'm really a very good cook."

Marsh looked pleased. "That's an offer I can't refuse. Thanks."

Abruptly, his expression became serious and he added, "But don't feel guilty because you were upset. I'm glad I was here for you. You're too hard on yourself, Kim. It took a lot of courage to leave all your friends behind, move up here, live in this big house all alone.

"And when someone has been living with sustained stress, going as hard as they can, day after day, just to keep one step ahead of things, when the time comes to stop, everything has a way of catching up.

"So if your nerves get the better of you sometimes —well, you're entitled!" He stopped speaking, laughed self-consciously. "End of sermon."

I didn't say anything. I couldn't. It was so wonderful to know he understood. I gave him a tremulous smile.

We both stood up then, and Marsh laid his hand on my arm, "Tell you what," he said, "I was going to ask you to drive me back to town since I don't have a spare tire, but maybe you'd feel safer if I stayed here tonight."

"Oh, would you!" I couldn't mask the relief in my voice, didn't try. I felt as if a huge load had been lifted from my shoulders.

"It's all settled," he assured me, then added, "And if you like, while you're getting something ready to eat, I'll go up and get the fires going in the bedrooms. It'll take the chill off before bedtime."

"Thanks. I hate undressing in a cold room."

"Me too," he said with a sheepish grin. "I've never been keen on roughing it."

I laughed. "How nice to meet an honest man," I said, then added, "I think you'd be most comfortable in the back bedroom, the one next to the bath. You'll even find a new toothbrush and some other things you might need. . . ."

We left the parlor together, each carrying a lamp, but I turned right, toward the kitchen, and Marsh went off to the left, up the backstairs to the bedrooms on the second floor.

It wasn't until much later, after I was in bed; was, in fact, just falling asleep, that I began to wonder, and not for the first time, how it was Marsh seemed so at home in this great house. It wasn't just that he appeared to know his way around, it was the easy familiarity he obviously felt. And the footsteps I had heard in the hall. He had explained them so glibly; but I knew those footsteps had come down the hall, had stopped at the parlor door—could Marsh have run quietly back up the hall, lighted the lamp again, then made a second appearance? But to what purpose? I covered my ears with my palms as if I could shut out the sound of my own thoughts.

I was certain I was too upset, too plagued by unanswerable questions to sleep, but sleep at last I did, and it was only in my dreams that I heard someone calling my name. "David?" I answered. "David! Is that you?" But it was only a dream.

# ELEVEN

The following morning dawned warm, bright, and clear. Yesterday's unseasonable cold had followed the storm clouds inland, and as soon as I wakened, I rose and dressed, thinking to precede Marshall downstairs. But I found that he had risen even earlier than I and already had the cats fed, a pot of coffee perking, and breakfast ready to put on the table. Obviously the electricity had been restored.

Marsh grinned rather sheepishly when I entered the kitchen. "Hope you don't mind . . . as a self-invited guest, thought maybe I could earn my keep by fixing breakfast."

Our eyes met, clung for a moment, then Marshall glanced quickly away and a bit of the brightness flowed out of the day. It surprised me to realize how much I wanted Marsh's approval, wanted him to like me; but each time we seemed to be drawing near one another, he closed himself in, locked himself away from me. Why? I wondered. Was it me? Did he really feel nothing for me? Had I only imagined that closeness we had shared the first day we met?

His voice interrupted my thoughts. "Are you hungry?" Again his eyes met mine for an instant, and I realized with a little thrill of pleasure that they were aglow with happiness. No sadness there today.

I smiled and, twitching my nose, I leaned slightly forward sniffing the savory aroma of fresh-brewed coffee and frying bacon. "If it tastes as good as it smells, I'll offer you the job on a permanent basis," I promised.

He handed me a glass of juice and urged me toward the table. "Sit down . . . everything's ready."

We settled down and ate in silence for a few moments, then Marshall asked, "Did you sleep well?"

Actually, my sleep had been troubled. Propelled by nightmarish dreams, I had tossed and turned much of the night; but I smiled and replied, "Like a log."

"Good," Marshall nodded. "If you like, soon as we finish breakfast, I'll see if I can locate the furnace. Maybe I can get it started before I leave."

"Do you think you should?" I gave him a dubious glance, wondering if he really understood the mysteries of a furnace.

"No problem," he assured me.

When we had finished our last cup of coffee, Marsh stood up and said, "Let me have a look at the basement."

I gazed at him in consternation, then shook my head. "I don't know where . . ."

For a long moment, we contemplated each other in silence. Finally Marshall said, "I think there's an outside entrance around back. I'll go have a look."

By the time Marsh returned, I had the kitchen in order once more. He shook his head as he walked in. "Couldn't find it." He shrugged. "Can't understand it. There's got to be a basement."

"Never mind," I said. "Stephen . . . Mr. Enders is sure to know where it is."

Marsh's eyebrows raised slightly, but he said nothing, only nodded.

"Another cup of coffee?" I offered.

He shook his head. Apparently his mind was still busy with the problem of the furnace. "I did find the woodshed out back of the garage and I brought in some logs."

"Oh, thanks . . . that's great."

"Now, is there anything else I can do for you before you run me back to town?"

I shook my head, no.

"While I was outside, I took off my flat tire and put it in your car, so if you're ready . . . ?"

I glanced out the window. "Will I need a sweater? It looks so beautiful out there."

He smiled. "It is. Like a day in spring but you'd be smart to bring a wrap. The weather can be tricky here in the Pacific Northwest, especially this time of year."

The ride into town was lovely. Like aged rulers clothed in gracious green, drooping hemlock and stately spruce with diadems of burgeoning cones stood unbending while all about them crowds of dogwood and aspen in their autumnal robes of russet and brown danced attendance on the shy maple in its veil of vermillion and yellow and gold. Lower-growing shrubs and vines were heavy with chains of bright red berries and the Canadian thistle wore crowns of shimmering silver.

We rode in silence most of the way, each of us lost in our own thoughts. However, as we drew near the village, I became acutely aware of Marshall's eyes upon me and I turned to smile at him.

His face remained sober. "What you were telling me last night . . ." he began, "about the noises . . ." His voice trailed away.

I turned my attention back to the road. "Probably just my imagination," I said. When he made no comment I added, "Or something with a perfectly natural explanation."

He remained silent, and I glanced at him again. He was still looking at me thoughtfully, but when our eyes met, he smiled.

"I don't want to frighten you . . . all the same, it wouldn't hurt to be careful. Maybe you should get a dog. . . ."

I was taken aback by his comment. Did he really think I was in danger? Or did he simply believe I would find the presence of a dog reassuring?

I was determined not to let my overwrought imagination get the best of both of us. "Oh, I'm sure I'll be all right," I assured him. Driving through that wonderful golden morning with Marsh beside me, all the fear of the night just past seemed far away. Besides, Marsh had understood, and somehow, his concern served to restore my own sense of self-reliance.

In town, I dropped Marshall off at the garage, and despite his assurance that he could take a cab back to Wiffen Cove, I told him I would pick him up on my way home.

His eyes considered me thoughtfully. Then he said, his voice sober, "Only if you'll let me take you to lunch first."

I laughed. "You make it sound like a threat . . .

but I think lunch would be very nice, though it's really not necessary."

"I know, but I'd like to."

"Then I'd like to, too."

"Now," he said, looking a bit sheepish, "if you could just drop me by my room . . ."

"At the Sea Urchin Motel."

He looked surprised. "How did you know?"

"I haff my vays," I said, trying to look mysterious.

"You mean, it's the only motel in town." He laughed.

When we reached the motel I glanced at my watch. I'll pick you up about eleven-thirty . . . O.K.?"

"O.K.," he agreed.

After leaving Marshall, I drove directly to the office of Enders and Enders, but the CLOSED sign was still in the window. How very odd, I thought. I wondered if perhaps I should try to reach Vera at home, but decided against it. After all, I reasoned, she must have many friends who will be concerned if she is ill or something. I sighed. Despite my show of bravado when talking to Marsh, the terror I had experienced the night before had left me more anxious than ever to find a roomer.

Next, I went to the post office. There was only one letter in my box, a note from Stephen. It was a reminder that we had a date for Friday night. "I'll pick you up about seven," it said. "Be prepared for a gala evening." At the bottom, under the signature, he had added, "I miss you!"

I smiled to myself and a warm contented feeling glowed inside me. I had forgotten how reassuring it could be to have a handsome man interested in you.

And, I thought, Stephen is certainly one very hand-some man.

I still had half an hour to kill before picking up Marshall and impulsively I walked up the street to an art supply store on the corner. Inside, it was cool and quiet. I glanced about looking for the display of oil paints. I had made a list the day before of those colors that were low and of other things that I would need if I were to start painting seriously again; but I had left the list lying on the lamp table next to the Queen Anne rocker. "Botheration!" I said softly.

A voice at my shoulder asked, "May I help you?"

Startled, I spun about, almost bumping into the young woman I had seen at the post office the previous day.

"Oops. Sorry about that," she said.

I shook my head though my heart was pounding. "It's just that I didn't hear you coming."

"It's these shoes." She held up one of her feet. "They have crepe soles. They're great when you have to be on your feet all day . . . but I do seem to sneak up on a lot of customers."

My smile felt a bit shaky. "Do they all jump like I just did?"

She nodded, mischief sparkling in her eyes. "A lot of them do." Then she laughed, "Maybe I should hang a bell around my neck." Her face sobered. "Is there something I can help you with?"

"I do need some oils . . . other things, too; but I forgot my list." I had selected several tubes of paint while we talked, and now we started up the aisle together.

She suggested several other items, but I shook my

head. "I think I'll just let it go until next time when I have my list."

After I had paid for my purchases, the young woman said, "We get a lot of artists here on the island. They seem to like the light."

I nodded. Although I hadn't consciously remarked it, I remembered the way the planes of light and shadow had seemed almost to shimmer the day I had tried to paint the Tor.

"I can see by your expression that you've noticed it." Her tone of voice told me she was pleased that I understood what she was trying to say.

"Yes," I agreed. "The light does have a special lucidity."

"And our way of life here on the islands . . . quiet and relaxed . . . seems to appeal to people." Her voice betrayed her pride.

I smiled inwardly. Thus far, I thought, I have found it neither quiet nor relaxing, and I commented wryly, "Except for the occasional murder or drowning, you mean?"

Her eyes widened and she stared at me for a moment nonplussed. Then she said, "Oh, God, I'm sorry. I guess I shouldn't have told you about that. . . ."

I shrugged. "Never mind. It would have come out sooner or later. I guess I should thank you for telling me. No one else did."

She brightened perceptibly. "From now on, the news will all be good. I promise."

I laughed. "Not to change the subject," I said, "but do we have any well-known artists living here on our island?"

She shook her head. "Right here, no. But several

very well-known people make their homes on San Juan and Lopez . . . Guemes, too . . . the larger islands mostly. And not just painters. You should visit La Conner. Actually, it's a channel town; but there are some fine galleries there: pottery, sculptures, jewelry, batikes . . . all created by our islanders. I know you'd enjoy it."

"I'm sure I would. I'll make a point of visiting some of the other islands as soon as I'm settled."

She nodded and smiled shyly. "We have our own art fair here each summer."

"Really? That sounds like fun. Is it just for professionals or can . . . ?"

She shrugged. "Well, to be honest, mostly amateurs. But some of our participants have had private showings, and several have gained rather a wide following." She hesitated, then added quickly, "Maybe you could get some of your things ready to show."

"Do you really think I should?" I asked, but I was already running over in my mind the pictures I had that might be suitable.

So engrossed was I in our conversation, I had completely forgotten the time. It wasn't until another customer walked in that I glanced at my watch. It was already a quarter to twelve. "Oh, darn!" I exclaimed. "I had an eleven-thirty appointment. I must run; but maybe we can talk more one day next week."

"I'll look forward to seeing you," she called after me.

I hurried back to my car and drove to Marshall's motel as quickly as I could. He was out in front, walking slowly up and down, his head bowed. I pulled up to the curb beside him, leaned over and opened the door. "Sorry I'm late," I called. "I was talking to the young woman at the art supply house and lost track of the time."

He slid into the seat beside me. "That must have been Rosemary. Her folks own the store but she runs it." He had changed into a pair of tan slacks and a brown tweed sport coat. His hair was still damp from the shower and an elusive scent of pine soap and aftershave followed him.

I put the car in gear. "Well, where to?" I asked.

"Have you been to the Longhouse out at Deadman's Cove yet?"

"Deadman's Cove?" I repeated. "Sounds like a charming spot."

He laughed. "It really is."

I eased the car away from the curb. "Just tell me how to get there."

"That's the spirit. . . ."

"Don't tell me," I said. "The spirit of Deadman's Cove."

Marsh groaned. "I'm going to pretend you never said that. In fact, I'm going right on with my tour guide recitation."

"Thank you and please do," I said. I could feel his eyes studying me and I longed to turn and look at him, but the road curved and twisted ahead of us.

After a pause, Marsh continued. "The restaurant is owned by the local Indian tribe and the food is good. Not fancy, but good."

The Longhouse proved to be just what its name implied; a long, rectangular, one-story, log building. From the outside, it was without character or interest; but within its four walls was another world. I gazed in awe at the beautiful, handwoven rugs that hung upon the walls, and after we were seated, my eyes sought out the intricately patterned, handwoven baskets that were artfully displayed throughout the room as were amulets of shell, feather, fur, and leather. In the center of the room, a magnificent totem pole thrust its head against the rafters above.

A young woman with jet black hair and lustrous black eyes showed us to a table near the back wall and gave us each a menu. The choices were limited, but fresh barbecued salmon was the house specialty.

"It's the best barbecued salmon in the state," Marsh declared.

After we had ordered, Marshall said, "Everything you see here is created locally. You probably guessed that the rugs and baskets are handwoven, but few people guess that the dyes they use are still made in the traditional way from herbs and berries and shellfish; leather and fur are tanned right here; beads and figurines are all handcarved; jewelry is handcrafted."

I gazed slowly about the room, my eyes lingering on first one piece and then another. "These things are lovely. That basket with the fish motif . . . and that rug . . . Is it all the work of the local tribe?"

My gaze returned to Marsh's face and his eyes began to dance. "All except the totem," he said. "That's the work of a white man."

I shook my head. "Oh, come on, Marsh, that's the most, uh, *Indian* thing here!"

"No, I'm not kidding. A gentleman who lived in Anacortes for many years took an interest in totem carving. He knew it was becoming a lost art. So he taught himself all there was to know about totems, wrote a book on the subject, and became the leading carver of totem poles here in the Pacific North-west."

"What a lovely story. I'd like to read the book."

Marsh looked pleased. "I have a copy. You can borrow it anytime you like."

When we emerged from the Longhouse, we found the sun was warm and the sky a glorious gentian blue overhead. "Let's walk down to the cove," Marshall suggested and I nodded agreement.

We followed a narrow path that was almost over-grown by vines and thickets of fern. Birds trilled overhead and somewhere nearby a small creature scuttled for safety. As we rounded a curve in the trail, an enormous-looking, striped snake slithered smoothly away into the undergrowth.

Startled, I took a quick step backward, half-turned, and fell against Marsh. Instinctively his arms closed about me. His eyes looked into mine, his breath caressed my cheek, his lips closed gently over my own, and the whole world stood still.

Happiness flowed through me. I relaxed against his chest, could feel his heart pounding in rhythm with mine; and I felt at peace. I felt warm and happy and safe . . . the way I had felt in David's arms.

Abruptly, he released me, turned away. "I'm sorry," he said, "I shouldn't have done that." His voice was quiet, controlled.

I stared at him.

He wasn't smiling. His dark eyes looked stormy—almost angry—but his voice was calm as he contin-ued, "That little garter snake couldn't hurt you. I took advantage of the situation."

I didn't understand. Why was he rejecting me? Suddenly, I felt such a fool; but I tried to be as casual as he seemed to be. "No harm done." I laughed. "There's nothing wrong with a kiss between friends."

He nodded, then quickly changed the subject. "We're almost there now. Feel like going on?"

The cove was small and closely surrounded by a thick stand of evergreens. The tide was out. The tiny beach was a welter of moss-covered rock and driftwood all laced together with long strands of seaweed and kelp. A stiff breeze blew in from the strait, cold and damp, laden with the sharp, clean, briny scent of saltwater.

"It is lovely," I murmured, "but so lonely. . . ." And the shiver that coursed through me was not entirely from the cold.

Marshall was silent, his eyes fixed on the horizon. At length he said softly, "That's the Pacific out there, out beyond the strait. In the old days, smugglers brought in everything from aliens to whiskey and wool." He sighed. "And if the authorities got too close, they just dumped whatever they were carrying overboard."

"Even the aliens?" I had read about such things, but hearing Marsh say the words gave reality to the idea, a reality that was both frightening and shocking.

Marsh turned his gaze on me, as if he were searching for something in my face. "That's how this cove got its name . . . from the bodies that used to wash ashore here. . . ."

I winced. "That's a pretty ugly story. . . ."

"Smuggling's an ugly business. . . ."

Marsh's eyes continued to appraise me. The breeze was really cutting into me by then and again I shivered. "You're cold." Marshall's tone was contrite. "I'd best be getting you home."

The ride back to town was uneventful. We stopped and picked up his tire and were back at Wiffen Cove by four o'clock. I sat on the steps and we chatted while Marshall changed the tire.

When he was finished, I said, "How about some coffee?"

But he declined. "Thanks," he said, "but I've really got to get back to work. Believe it or not, I do have a job."

Suddenly, I realized Marshall had never mentioned what he did for a living; in fact, had never told me anything at all about himself. He had a knack for getting me to talk about myself, but the only things he had ever revealed about himself had to do with his childhood and his friendship with Sylvia.

As these thoughts flickered through my mind, he started the car's engine, put it in gear, and with a wave of his hand, was gone. I was alone.

Slowly, I walked out onto the lawn, turned, looked up at the house. Sinister, dark, and cold, a malign monster, it loomed over me. And the temptation to jump into my car and drive away as fast as I could was almost overpowering. But I resisted, standing there, trembling slightly, trying to calm myself. I don't know what I would have done had not Clarence come bounding across the grass to curl himself around my ankles, purring loudly. Somehow his presence eased the tension.

I picked him up and buried my cheek in his soft

fur. His purr became a sonorous growl in my ear and I gave him a hug. "You'll protect me, won't you, Clare?" I whispered.

However, I still could not bring myself to open those huge double doors and walk through the silent rooms, the long, dark hall to the kitchen. Instead, I returned to the walkway, circled around to the back, and entered through the servants' entrance. Stephen had told me that was what Sylvia always called the back door.

I put Clarence on the floor in the kitchen and sat down at the table. Sheba came out of the Port-a-Pet, hissed at Clare, then sat down beside him. Cleo pushed her nose through the cat door and joined the other two. There they sat, staring up at me with expectant eyes.

I shook my head. "Surely you're not hungry again?"

Clarence began to prance, Sheba offered a complaint-filled "Maooo," and Cleo jumped onto my knees and leaned her chin upon my breast.

"O.K., O.K." I laughed, rising and going to the cupboard. I filled their dishes and put them on the floor. As they began to eat, I crossed to the window and looked out. The shadows from the taller trees were halfway across the lawn, and the waters of the strait were burnished by the coppery light from the setting sun.

The nervous dread I had held at bay ever since Marshall drove away moved closer. How quiet the house was. Too quiet. I started to turn around and realized I was afraid to move. I was even holding my breath, lest the sound of my breathing should disclose my presence in the house. A moment longer

I stood frozen, then I whirled about—there was nothing there, but the hair on the back of my neck still crawled and I moved away from the window, sat once more at the table.

What am I going to do? I asked myself. I'm being so silly! There's nothing here to hurt me. I reminded myself that Sylvia had lived in the house alone for the better part of ten years—nothing had ever hurt her. Marshall had assured me the rumors about a murder were just that—rumors. The police were satisfied that she had fallen down the stairway after taking an overdose of something. When I had pointed out that bruises don't form once the heart stops beating, Marsh only shrugged. "She must have bumped into something earlier in the day. It was a terrible accident, but just that: an accident."

I tried to accept his explanation, but my mind continued to reprocess the facts. An overdose of something—dust and bruises—an overdose . . . there had been dust on my face and a bruise on my arm—and my mouth had been so dry. The telephone had not wakened me—an overdose of something. . . .

Shadows were beginning to gather in the corners and under the chairs. Moving stiffly, like an automaton, I got up, turned on the light, and warmed myself a bowl of soup. By the time I had finished eating, it was dark outside the window, and I decided to go straight upstairs to bed. I told myself it was because I was tired; but I knew it was because I was afraid—afraid to go down the hall alone, afraid to sit in the parlor alone—and the later it got, the more afraid I would be; more afraid to climb the stairs to the second floor—more afraid to enter my dark bed-room—afraid—afraid. . . .

I tiptoed out into the hall. I did not turn out the kitchen light; neither did I turn on the light in the hallway. I had given up trying to get the cats to go upstairs with me, so now I hurried to the stairway alone and started up. How dark it was on the land-ing above me. My steps slowed, my heart pounded. I pressed myself against the wall and forced myself to continue upward.

When I reached the top step, I stood on tiptoe and my fingers groped the wall above my head until I found and flipped the light switch. A soft radiance that only served to accentuate the gloom, to deepen the shadows in the corners, flooded the hallway.

Fervently wishing I had remembered to exchange that twenty-watt bulb for something brighter, I stood transfixed, staring into the darkness. Nothing stirred. The area was empty save for the towering Sheraton wardrobe that stood at the end of the gal-lery, and, set at intervals along the wall, the Chip-pendale torchères holding their silver candlesticks.

But the door to my room stood open! Surely I had closed it that morning when I left! I had run back upstairs to get a sweater, and I had closed that door very carefully behind me when I went back down— or had I? The harder I tried to remember, the more nebulous the memory became. But, I told myself, I always close doors. I have a thing about closing doors and drawers—but maybe I forgot. . . .

I licked my lips, looked back down the stairway to the dark, forbidding hallway below, then looked once more at the open bedroom door. My fear of the darkness below proved to be the stronger. I

clenched my hands, squared my shoulders, and
moved purposefully toward the door. Before passing through it, I reached around the door frame and
flipped the light switch, then stuck my head inside,
peered about.

The scent of lavender was unmistakable—and
abruptly I realized it always seemed to pervade that
room. But it had been so faint, I had not recognized
it before. It seemed stronger tonight. My glance flew
from corner to corner and then, more slowly,
searched every inch, looking for some sign of an
interloper.

At first, everything appeared to be normal, yet different. What was it? I asked myself. Why did the
room look strange? Then, slowly, I began to take
note: the flowers that had been on the table in the
alcove were now on my nightstand; my robe was
not on the chair where I had left it, it was lying
across the foot of my bed; and the closet door stood
open!

My breath grew short, my knees felt weak. I
leaned against the wall for support. Could someone
be hiding right now under my bed? or lurking in the
dressing room? or in the bath? Should I run back
downstairs? But what if *it* had already gone downstairs and was waiting for me there?

Damn you, David, I thought, why did you have to
die and leave me alone! Anger flashed through me
like a blaze of light, then subsided as quickly as it
had risen. I knew all too well that David had not
chosen to leave me. But it wasn't my fault either, I
thought. The police had said it wasn't my fault. The
other driver had been drinking—his car had
swerved into my lane. . . .

And then the idea that had almost driven me crazy, day in day out, ever since the accident: if I hadn't insisted David let me drive . . .

I shook my head, pushed the idea back into my subconscious, forced my attention to return to the present; but somehow, the sudden skewing of thought had lessened my terror.

It's your damned imagination! I railed at myself. You moved those flowers, and your robe, and everything else yourself. You just don't remember— THERE'S NOTHING HERE TO HURT YOU!

Woodenly, I forced myself to stand up straight; pressed my hands, one over the other, hard against my solar plexis, and walked over to the closet. I peered carefully inside, then closed the door. Next I went to the bathroom and looked about, even pulled aside the shower curtain. Nothing. Last of all I returned to the bedroom, knelt down, and peered under the bed. Only a lonely dust bunny.

Assured that I had the room entirely to myself, I returned to the door, closed and locked it. Then, back to the bathroom to change into my nightie, but when I returned to my bed, I did not turn out the bathroom light.


I woke with a start. My room was filled with murky shadows. I was wide awake but I felt disoriented; there was something different. Something wrong. I lay quite still, staring up into the darkness, wondering, until I remembered: I had left the bathroom light burning. Now it was dark and there was something . . .

Dear God! I thought, as a paroxysm of fear shook me. Now I could hear it quite clearly; from somewhere nearby, out of the inky blackness came the unmistakable sound of breathing.

# TWELVE

~

**M**y heart lurched, a painful thud against my ribs, then began to pound so heavily, it was difficult to hear; but it seemed to me that the gentle susurration was drawing nearer. Soft and regular, the inhalation rather more pronounced than the exhalation.

For one infinite moment, my thoughts fluttered wildly about my brain like frightened birds in a small cage. Reason told me to flee, terror held me motionless; reason told me to scream, terror stopped the sound in my throat; reason told me to seek the light and a weapon, terror turned my arms and legs to jelly. Fear had become a physical thing, trapping me more certainly than chains of iron.

Then something brushed against the foot of the bed. The shock catapulted me into action. With a shriek of terror, I literally threw myself from the bed and did not stop moving until I was in the bathroom with the door locked behind me. Trembling, my breath gasping in my throat, I leaned against the door.

I had not yet caught my breath when a frenzied pounding on my bedroom door sent another wave of panic through me; but at the same time, I recognized Marsh's voice calling my name. But before I could pull myself together and respond, something hit the door with a heavy thud followed by the sound of splintering wood. Immediately thereafter, Marsh's voice came to me through the bathroom door.

"Kim! Kim, are you in there? Answer me or I'll break this damn door down, too."

"No . . . no, I'm all right." My voice was so weak I was not certain he could hear me, but I began immediately fumbling with the lock, trying to open the door.

Then it was open and I was in his arms. Tears of fear and relief were streaming down my face and great shuddering sobs wracked my chilled body.

Marsh picked me up and carried me to the bed. Somehow, without dropping me, he managed to strip off a comforter and wrap it snugly around me before carrying me down the stairs. In the kitchen, he sat me in a chair, then poured me a large shot of brandy, which I swallowed in one gulp. It burned all the way down and, though I could not stop shaking, it did help me to bring my sobbing under control.

"It's shock," Marsh said soothingly. "Just try to relax." As he talked, he put some milk on the stove to warm, and when it was ready, he made me drink that, too. Then he picked me up once more and carried me into the parlor where we had had tea the night before. First he laid me gently on the sofa, then pulled a small electric heater near and turned it on.

Clarence, who had followed us from the kitchen, jumped up beside me and curled himself into a round fuzzy ball in the small of my back while Cleo, miraculously appearing from the shadows, spread herself across my feet and began to hum a tiny contented song. Marsh pulled a hassock close and sat down beside us. He smoothed the disheveled curls back off my forehead with gentle fingers, then took my hands in both of his.

"Feeling better?" His eyes searched my face and I smiled—or tried to.

"Feel like talking about it? What happened?"

I shuddered, remembering. "There was someone in my room."

He watched me intently as I spoke; his face calm and grave. "Did you see someone?"

"No. I woke up and it was dark. I heard someone breathing."

"You're sure?"

"Yes . . . yes . . . I'm certain. I left the light on in the bathroom, but when I woke up, the light was out and I could hear someone breathing. . . ."

"Do you always leave the bathroom light on?"

"No . . . but when I went up to bed I noticed someone had been in my room. . . ."

He patted my hand, absently. Though his eyes were fixed on my face, his gaze seemed to be turned inward. At last he said, "Your door was locked from the inside, Kim. I had to break it down to get in." He smiled apologetically. "The lock must be ruined . . . probably the door frame as well."

I stared at him while his words took on meaning in my still foggy mind. "But I know . . ." The words dribbled away as another idea came into my mind. "How did you . . . I mean, why were you . . . ?"

He took a deep breath, released my hands, and

ran his fingers through his own tousled hair. "Well, last night, I got to thinking about the things you told me . . . about the way the cats were acting and the strange noises. I began to worry about you. I decided to come back out here and keep an eye on things. Actually, I was just outside when I heard you scream."

He had cared enough to come back. Such a small thing, really, yet I found the idea very comforting. But I had another question. "How how did you get in?"

"Jimmied the back door with a credit card. You could have me arrested for breaking and entering."

"No, no . . . thank God you were here!"

We were both silent for a while, each lost in our own thoughts. The grandfather clock in the observatory chimed three and Clarence began to snore peacefully.

Finally I asked, "Do you think I'm in some kind of danger?"

He shrugged. "I don't know, Kim, but I learned a long time ago to listen to my hunches. I just felt like you might need me tonight, so I came back."

It didn't occur to me then to ask why he hadn't just come back the night before and told me he thought he should be there—that I needed protection. I was too busy savoring the thought that he must care more for me than his earlier actions had indicated. So I only repeated, "Thank God you did come back." Suddenly my eyes felt very heavy and I realized how tired I was.

Marsh leaned forward, brushed his lips across my cheek. "Try to sleep," he murmured. "I'll be right here. . . ."

I don't remember falling asleep; but I woke to the sound of raindrops splattering on the windowpane. Clarence was gone, but Cleo was still lying across my feet making it difficult for me to move. Marsh was sleeping nearby in a large wingback chair, his neck twisted at an ungainly angle, his head resting against a small velvet cushion. Sheba, who had wedged herself down into the chair seat beside him, gurgled gently.

Even as I watched, Marsh's eyelids fluttered. Gingerly, he sat up, stretched, and began rubbing the back of his neck, but Sheba didn't move.

"Good morning," I said.

Marsh heaved himself to his feet and smiled down at me. "And how are you this morning?"

I, too, sat up and stretched. "A bit stiff, but otherwise fine." I wriggled out of the comforter and stood up.

Marshall's eyes opened appreciatively and I realized I was still clad only in the sheer nylon and lace gown I had worn to bed the night before. I could feel my cheeks blaze crimson and I grabbed up the comforter again, flung it about me.

"Shall I run upstairs and get you a robe or something?" Marshall didn't smile, but the tip of his nose had turned white.

I pulled the comforter closer and said haughtily, "Thank you, no. I'll go up and get dressed. I'm sure I'll be safe enough now that it's daylight."

Marsh, his smile reflex again under control, nodded. "I'll put on a pot of coffee if you like."

Later, over breakfast, I told Marsh exactly what had happened the night before.

He listened without comment, nodding his head

from time to time, and when I had finished my recital he asked, "Do you like this place, Kim? Do you really want to stay here?"

It seemed an odd question and something in his tone made me uneasy. "Why? What do you mean?"

"I mean, is there some other reason . . . some special reason for staying on here at Wiffen Cove?"

I stared at him, wondering what he was getting at. Finally I said, "Because I want to, of course."

His eyes remained fixed on me, his gaze clear and steady.

Without meaning to, I blurted, "Well, that's not entirely true. According to Aunt Sylvia's will, I can live here and receive an income from a trust fund as long as I live. But if I leave, I lose everything. To be honest, I've nowhere else to go. By the time David died, we were not only broke, I was in debt."

"If you leave here, who gets the property?"

"I don't know. I think it reverts to the State of Washington and the income from the trust goes to some art foundation."

"So no one in particular would profit from scaring you away?"

I shook my head. "I don't think so."

He took a deep breath, then said softly, "This old house is big and probably scary when you're here alone. Could it be that you . . ."

"You think I'm just imagining things?"

He sighed, shook his head. Sheba chose that moment to make her presence known, providing a welcome distraction. We finished breakfast discussing my cats' personalities. Then we took our coffee back to the parlor and settled ourselves, side by side, on the sofa.

Marsh was the first to speak. He seemed to be choosing his words with great care. "Have you any idea who could be doing this to you?"

The question startled me. Until that moment, I had not thought of the events that had so frightened me as part of a plot. In my mind, each incident had remained completely impersonal—like an earthquake or an avalanche—events that are dangerous and threatening, but not planned acts of violence directed against any one individual.

When I did not answer, Marsh turned and looked at me; but I only shook my head.

"Then have you thought about *why* anyone would want to scare you . . . hurt you?"

Again I shook my head, then added, "I don't know anyone here on the island except people I have met since I arrived: you, Vera and Stephen Enders, Tom and Claire Moss, Helen Riley." I pressed my fingertips against my temples, aware of a nagging pain beginning to pulse there. "And the girl in the art supply store." I turned my head and looked at Marsh. "I didn't even know Aunt Sylvia."

"Think about them, Kim. Has any one of them said or done anything you would consider out of the ordinary?"

After carefully considering each one in turn, I said, "Not really. Vera is an odd sort—sometimes friendly, sometimes not. She tried to persuade me to stay away from here, but that was because she thought it wasn't safe for me to be way out here all alone." I paused, then added, "Maybe she was right."

Marsh made no comment, so I continued, "And

I've run into that woman from the art store several times—"

Marsh interrupted, "Name's Rosemary Church. We went to school together."

"Anyway," I continued, "she's spoken to me several times, and always with something negative to say about this place. But she certainly didn't seem threatening."

A silence fell between us then. Marsh was obviously lost in thought, his eyes full of shadows, fixed on nothing. At last, slowly, he turned to gaze at me. "What about Marjory Blake?"

His words, his expression, sent a chill down my back. "Marjory Blake?" I parroted.

When he continued to stare at me, I said, "I only met her once. Well, didn't really meet her. Just passed her on the stairs that night. She spoke to Stephen, but no one introduced us."

Once more Marsh fell into a reverie. When he spoke again, it was to say, "Well, what about the why? Why would anyone, even a stranger, want to hurt you?"

The sadness had crept back into his eyes, and I wanted to reach out and touch his cheek, but I only shook my head. "I don't know . . . there isn't any reason. . . ."

Marshall sighed. "Tell me again about the note."

I rose quickly to my feet. "I'll do better than that. Excuse me for a moment and I'll show it to you." So saying, I left the room, dashed upstairs, and retrieved the yellow foolscap with its ominous message from the back of my "jewel" case, where I had shoved it the day it came.

Marshall read it, then asked, "Where's the envelope it came in?"

My face must have shown my surprise because he added, "Without the envelope, this could have come from anywhere, been written by anyone . . . even you."

If he had slapped me, I couldn't have been more shocked, and remembering my earlier misgivings, I snapped, "You do think I'm just making all this up!"

"I didn't say that. But think about it, Kim. If I take you to the sheriff to report that someone is harassing . . . threatening you, he'll want to know exactly how. He'll want to know all the details, and he'll want to see some real evidence. What can you tell him, show him, that can be backed up by hard cold facts?"

"I'm not making it up!" I said stubbornly.

Suddenly, Marsh stood up and began pacing about the room. "Look, I'm only trying to help; I'm not accusing you of anything but we have to consider all the possibilities." He came back to the sofa, stood looking down at me. Then he offered me his hand and said, "Come on, let's go back upstairs and search your room. Maybe we can find something."

We left the parlor, walked down the hall and up the stairs in silence. A glance confirmed Marsh's earlier concern: the door to my bedroom hung at a most precarious angle. Not only had he burst the lock in his assault upon it, he had destroyed the hinges as well.

Marshall pulled the door loose and leaned it against the wall before we stepped through the doorway. Inside, we stopped and looked carefully around the room. Everything was just as it had been when I went to bed the night before.

Marsh left my side and walked slowly about the room, then he walked over to the bathroom and flipped the light switch. The light did not come on. He turned and looked at me. "Looks like maybe the bulb burned out."

"But it was brand new!"

Marsh removed the glass shade and unscrewed the bulb, held it close to his ear and gave it a little shake. "Filament's broken. . . ."

I turned and ran from the room. I could hear his footsteps on the stairs behind me as I hurried down the hall to the parlor. I was crying by the time he caught up with me. He put his hands on my shoulders and gently turned me about so that I was facing him, then put his fingers under my chin and raised my face to his.

At first I thought he was going to kiss me. I wanted him to kiss me. I felt lonely and desperate, and I wanted him to take me in his arms and hold me tight, tell me he believed me. We were standing so close together, I could feel the warmth radiating from his body, could smell the subtle essence of his aftershave, and my body yearned for the comfort of his. My lips parted in anticipation of his own; but he let his hands fall to his sides, stepped back a pace.

For a moment longer I stared at him, first in surprise, then in frustration and anger. I spun about and walked quickly to the window, stood staring blindly through tear-filled eyes at the steam-clouded window.

"I'm sorry, Kim, I . . ." His voice was strained.

"It's all right." My own voice was tight and shallow.

"No, it isn't all right. I want to help you, but . . ."

I took a deep breath, clenched my hands into fists, and turned to face him, head held high. "Don't bother, Mr. Thorne. I think you have made your position quite clear."

He took a step toward me. "Kimberly, I . . ."

"I think you probably ought to leave now," I said, and I was surprised at how clear and controlled my voice sounded.

A moment longer he hesitated, then he said, "Perhaps you're right. I think you'll be safe enough today. I'll check with you later."

I only nodded, afraid to trust my voice further. Not until I was certain he had gone did I allow myself the comfort of tears. I threw myself down on the sofa and wept. I couldn't seem to think at all clearly: about what had happened, about Marshall Thorne, about how I felt. It had all become a muddle in my brain and somehow, though I couldn't think why, it was all my fault. Everything was my fault. If only I hadn't come to Wiffen Cove. Still wallowing in self-pity, I drifted off to sleep.

When I awoke, it was after three. My eyes and lips were puffy from crying and my head ached. I went back upstairs, took an aspirin, washed my face, and was just beginning to brush my hair when the door chimes sounded. Now what! I thought, irritation flaring. I didn't want to face anyone right at that moment; but the doorbell chimed insistently and I decided I'd best answer it.

It was Helen Riley. "Excuse me, miss," she said

pleasantly. "Mr. Thorne told me he thought you might be looking for some live-in help?"

Her words took me completely by surprise. Again, Marsh Thorne had managed to astonish me. He practically said he didn't believe my story, yet he had taken the trouble to find someone for me. To Helen, I said, "Do come in. Let's talk about it."

I brewed some tea and made some sandwiches; then we discussed arrangements. We agreed that in exchange for her room and board, she would take care of the cleaning and the laundry, and we would share the cooking. We also agreed that for the winter, at least, we would close off most of the rooms, thus lightening the cleaning load and lowering the heating bills. We also agreed that she should move in on Monday.

It wasn't until Helen remarked that that would give her the weekend to pack, that I remembered it was Friday and Stephen was going to pick me up at seven o'clock. I glanced at my watch. It was already five-thirty.

# THIRTEEN

Stephen would be there in less than two hours, and I promised myself, neither the events of the last few days nor my growing fear of the house itself should intrude upon this evening with him. Still smarting from Marsh's rejection, I was determined to prove how desirable I could be. So after a hot soaky bath, I dressed very carefully in the only formal gown I owned, a copy of a haute couture creation I had seen in a shop on Rodeo Drive in Beverly Hills. The original was of white silk, but I made my copy from a soft, clinging synthetic in a shimmering emerald green that highlighted the red in my hair and brought out the green in my eyes.

When I was ready, I surveyed my image in the full-length mirror, noting with satisfaction how flattering the gown was. When I pirouetted before the mirror, the intricately draped skirt swirled and eddied about my feet in a most satisfying way. I hummed an old dance tune, held out my arms, and took a few tentative steps. The gown rippled and flowed around me with a graceful, sensuous movement and, as I watched my own reflection in the mirror, beyond it, also reflected on the mirror's surface, I caught a glimpse of sinuous movement behind me.

I stopped dancing, then whirled about ready to face my attacker, only to find myself facing my own reflection in the alcove windows whose glistening surfaces had been turned into mirrors by the blackness outside. I released my breath in a long slow sigh. Night had fallen! Without warning, apprehension slid its cold fingers down my spine. I shivered, grabbed up my evening bag and my black wool coat, then hurried down the stairs.

Stephen arrived promptly at seven wearing a dinner jacket and bow tie. The deep tan he had acquired during the week he had been away accentuated the touch of gray at his temples, the clear steely gray of his eyes; and when he looked down at me, smiling a slow, intimate smile, my pulses began to race sending the hot blood coursing through me.

"How beautiful you are," he murmured, and the glow in his eyes confirmed the sincerity of his words.

The touch of his hand on my arm as he helped me into the car sent a tremor of awareness through me, and I again wondered, fleetingly, Am I falling in love with this man?

Stephen drove us directly to the small local landing strip. "We're taking the helicopter to Seattle. This is going to be a very special evening," he assured me.

"Oh, Stephen," I said, "how exciting! I've never flown in a helicopter before."

He smiled. "Good. I hope that from now on I can share a lot of the *firsts* in your life."

"What about my sharing some *firsts* in your life?" I teased.

He looked chagrined. "That, my dear young woman, would not be so easy."

I gazed intently into his face. Although his tone was light, there was something in his eyes: weariness—disillusion—regret? Was I being overly imaginative again? An unexpected chill raised goosebumps down my arms.

We didn't talk during the trip to the mainland; the noise of the copter engine precluded any exchange except at the top of one's voice. We landed at a small heliport on the waterfront and took a taxi to one of Seattle's best-known hotels.

Dinner was excellent. As always, Stephen ordered for me and selected the perfect wine. We laughed, we talked, we danced, and each time I turned to face Stephen on the dance floor I thought, How handsome he is. Later in the evening the band played some of the ballads from the forties and fifties. Stephen held me close, his cheek resting against the top of my head.

The music enveloped us, fused our movements, our emotions, our thoughts, and when Stephen whispered, "Shall we go?" I looked up into his eyes and smiled my acquiescence. Not until we were actually standing in a suite on the tenth floor did any misgivings reach the surface of my mind. Defiantly, I brushed them away; resolutely, gave my attention to my surroundings.

Thick pile carpeting in a soft shade of gray covered the floor. Sofas and chairs, deeply padded with velvet in a delicate shade of ivory that reflected the pearly overtones of the rug, were accented with throw cushions of assorted sizes and shapes, ranging in color from pale rosy pink to a deep coral.

Against one wall, an oriental lacquered cabinet stood, flanked by a large porcelain urn in which a dwarf plum tree grew, its branches covered with fragile pink blossoms. The opposite wall was constructed entirely of sliding glass doors that opened onto a narrow balcony overlooking the city and the sound. To my right, a marble-top bar, and to the left, through an open door, I could see into another lavishly furnished room.

Stephen closed the hall door, then came to stand close behind me. With one arm he encircled my waist, let his fingers gently knead my yielding flesh. With the fingers of his other hand, he caressed the column of my throat as he pulled me back against his chest.

I wondered if he could feel the nervousness trembling within me, and I tried to relax, tried to tell myself that this was what I wanted.

His thumb moved against my breast. "Do you like it?"

The breath caught in my throat.

Stephen laughed ever so softly, his breath stirred a tendril of hair behind my ear. "Our own decorator did this suite. . . ."

"It's beautiful. . . ."

But Stephen wasn't listening. He bent his head, and his lips began to move over my bare shoulder, delicate little kisses that I could scarcely feel, yet they were turning my body to flame. My head drooped back against his shoulder and those wonderful kisses followed the line of my throat, my jaw, found my ear, and he whispered, "I want you,

Kim . . ." while his fingers, gentle but sure, left my throat, moved downward, slipped inside the soft folds of my dress. His palm molded the fullness of my breast before he drew his fingers up to caress and fondle the eager roseate, tease it to a throbbing point.

Somehow, I forced myself to move a step away from him, to turn, to look up into his face. I took a deep breath, tried to speak firmly, but my words, when they came, were only a whisper, "I didn't come prepared to stay. . . ."

Stephen didn't move, his expression didn't change, but his eyes held mine. A tremor, whether of fear or excitement, I wasn't sure, flowed through me, and my knees felt weak.

Just the shadow of a smile flickered in Stephen's eyes. "Do you really want to leave?"

I licked my lips. "It must be very late. . . ." I was having difficulty breathing.

"Yes," he agreed. "Very late . . ."

For a moment I thought I detected a note of irony in his tone, but then he took me in his arms and pulled me close once more. The tip of his tongue caressed the shell of my ear and shivers of desire burst within me.

"I've wanted you from that first moment I saw you . . ." he breathed before his lips, possessive and demanding, closed over mine.

All my life, I believed that love and sex were more or less synonymous. It had never occurred to me that I could wildly desire someone I did not love. How wrong I had been! I hadn't been sure until that very moment how I felt about Stephen; but in that instant, when his lips closed over mine, setting a white hot passion ablaze within me, I knew that I didn't love him. He was handsome, charming, fascinating—all those things we women think we want in a man; but I knew I didn't love him.

But I wanted him to make love to me! My whole being blazed with a need beyond my ability to control. Even without my heart's consent, my body clamored for Stephen's touch.

I shouldn't let him kiss me, I thought, not like this. But I didn't draw away. I gave him kiss for passionate kiss as his hands moved down my back urging my body closer to his.

With a convulsive shudder of pleasure, I stopped thinking, gave myself up to the magic of his touch, sank willingly into the whirlpool of blazing sensation awakened by his fingers as they explored, caressed my eager flesh; and when his mouth left mine, began to wander over my face, my throat, I arched my body back and pulled his head down to my throbbing breasts. I was limp in his arms when he gathered me up and carried me into the bedroom.

As he lowered me to the bed, I reached out my arms to draw him close once more, but he resisted my embrace. Dimly, I became aware that the bedside telephone was ringing, its sound muffled but insistent.

Stephen pulled away from me. "I'm sorry, darling," he murmured, his voice a husky whisper. "I'd better answer . . . no one would call at this time of night if it weren't important."

He picked up the phone and I listened impatiently, but Stephen said little; and when he did re-

turn the receiver to its cradle, still he did not return
to me.

"Kim, darling . . . I'm sorry . . . I can't
stay. . . ."

Disbelieving, I opened my eyes and stared up at
the pale outline of his face in the predawn light.

"That phone call . . . I can't stay, but you sleep
as late as you wish."

Now I came fully alert, the shock of his words
spilling like ice water over my inflamed senses.
"You're leaving me here?" Surely, I had misunderstood.

"I'm sorry, darling. You're wonderful! I'd stay if I
could. . . ."

I listened in silence, my thoughts in turmoil.

"You can get anything you want or need from
room service . . . they'll put it on my account. And
when you are ready to leave, call the desk . . . I'll
leave instructions. The copter reservation and my
car keys are on the coffee table. I'll be out to Wiffen
Cove in a couple of days to pick up the car." Even as
he spoke, he slid out of bed and began to dress.

"Stephen, you . . ."

Abruptly, he leaned close once more, covered my
mouth with his own in a long, slow kiss that left me
weak and breathless. "Next time," he whispered,
"I'll make love to you all night and all day . . . but
now I must go."

After he had gone, I lay staring into the darkness,
wondering what could have happened, where he
could have gone. With the coming of dawn, I at first
considered getting up and leaving immediately, but
on second thought I liked Stephen. He had been
very good to me from the first day we had met.

Maybe I would learn to love him. It wouldn't be the way it had been with David that first wonderful year. But Stephen seemed to love me even if he had never said the words.

Now my thoughts returned to David and a chill settled over me. David. My David. I wondered if he knew that I was here, reveling in the memory of another man's arms?

But the sense of shame and guilt I had expected did not engulf me. Without warning, anger welled up and bitter tears stung the backs of my eyelids.

"Oh, David," I whispered, and curled myself into a ball of misery.

I must have cried myself to sleep because the bedside digital said ten-thirty when I awoke. But the tears had served their purpose. I was calm once more. I rolled over and stretched luxuriously. It occurred to me that I had never before slept between satin sheets, and I smiled lazily to myself. I wondered idly if Stephen realized just how many *firsts* he had shared with me.

I closed my eyes and for a moment forced myself to remember the feel of him, his body warm and hard, smooth as the satin sheets that lay against my body now. Would Stephen ask me to marry him? What would I say?

And suddenly, I found myself thinking of Marshall Thorne. Impatiently, I threw back the cover. What I needed was a shower. And still I lingered in that huge round bed, trying to understand my feelings. I had spent the night, well, almost spent the night, with a man who wasn't my husband—a man I didn't really love; or did I?

Stephen was always kind, thoughtful, generous.

Even though he had never said he loved me—maybe he was the kind of man who found those words difficult to say. Anyway, I probably did love him. It was foolish, I told myself, to expect a second love to be like the first. No man would ever take David's place.

Now, with the thought of David, Marsh's face intruded itself upon my consciousness. I recoiled as if I had been burned. I won't think of him . . . I just won't! I told myself.

I jumped as a rap sounded on the door followed immediately by a young woman's voice. "Room service."

I was too surprised to question this development. My response was automatic. "Come in."

The door opened and a maid stepped into the room pushing a serving cart. "Good morning, madam." She smiled. "Will you have your coffee in bed?"

I started to say no, then remembered I had nothing to put on. Quickly changing my mind, I nodded, "Yes, please."

She pushed the cart up within my reach and looked at me inquiringly.

"That's fine," I said, and suddenly I felt a warm blush suffusing my throat, my cheeks. Now, I thought, she'll know for sure I'm a scarlet woman, and the thought, though it made me giggle, served also to deepen the flame in my face.

The young woman's expression remained pleasantly impersonal. "Will there be anything else?" she asked.

"No, thank you."

As soon as the maid had gone, I swung my legs over the side of the bed and poured myself a steaming cup of the coffee. There was a pitcher of orange juice, two silver-covered dishes, and a warming tray on the cart as well as a rose and the morning paper. I raised the lid off the nearest dish and peeked in: eggs Benedict and sausage. Then I checked the warming tray: Danish pastries, blueberry muffins, and flaky croissants. The cart was also laden with silver dishes and bowls filled with gooseberry jam, strawberry preserves, bitter orange marmalade, and sweet butter served up in dainty curls.

I realized then that Stephen must have requested a morning call before he received the news that necessitated his departure. Or perhaps, the thought flashed through my mind, he has a standing order—breakfast for two whenever he . . .

I shook my head, unwilling to pursue that train of thought. Instead, I stood up, pulled a sheet off the bed, and draped it about me. The carpet was thick and soft beneath my bare feet as I pushed the cart over to a chair in front of the window. I seated myself, then glanced curiously around. I had been too preoccupied last night to notice all my surroundings. Oddly, I found that thought embarrassing.

However, it was a lovely room. Several small chairs and the huge round bed were covered with ivory satin brocade. The pale blue walls were hung with pastel prints taken from paintings by Matisse and Monet. A lovely French provincial wardrobe contained a large television and VCR.

Idly, I wondered why Stephen maintained a place like this. It must be dreadfully expensive, I thought. Obviously, he was a very successful man. Abruptly, the memory of Marjory in her gold lamé blouse blossomed in my mind. Was this what she had meant by her vulgar comment? Suddenly, the morning did not seem so bright.

The full-bodied aroma of the steaming coffee together with the fragrance of the fresh-squeezed juice reminded me that I was famished. Nonetheless, I took my time over my breakfast, trying to enjoy the view of the city and the sound. But beyond the window, the morning was gray beneath a high overcast, and a feeling of despondency began to grow deep down inside me. At last I pushed back my chair and stood up.

A hot shower is what I need, I assured myself; but I changed my mind when I entered the bathroom. It contained a large combination tub and sauna surrounded on three sides by plants and vines that seemed to thrive with the aid of artfully concealed grow-lamps. In a shallow niche above the tub I found a flagon of bubbling bath oil, soap, and shampoo.

So much for a shower, I thought, and ran myself a brimming tub liberally laced with bath oil. I lowered myself gratefully into the steaming bubbles and tried to relax; but even a half-hour of soaking in all that luxury did little to revive my spirits. In fact, I was so depressed by the time I climbed out of the tub, the realization that I had nothing to put on except the gown in which I had left home the evening before seemed almost funny. But I didn't laugh as I wrapped myself in a thick soft towel.

Back in the bedroom, I noted that it was growing late. It was time I got dressed and returned to Saturday Island. As I slipped into my evening finery, I thought, Thank goodness, I don't own an evening wrap. At least I have my old wool coat to cover my dress. But the coat didn't cover the long skirt. I'd have to find some way to tie it up if I were to leave the hotel with some semblance of respectability.

I went back into the bedroom and began opening drawers. It was immediately apparent that Stephen had spent—or intended to spend—a lot of time in the suite. The closets and chests were full: suits, shirts, shoes. I also found a surprising number of feminine garments. Vera must spend time here too, I thought, although they seemed a bit frilly for her. But who else? It was an uncomfortable question that I chose not to pursue.

In the end I took one of Stephen's neckties, tied it tightly around my waist, then hitched my gown up until it did not show beneath my coat. Ready at last, I took one final look around that beautiful, luxurious suite, then hurried out.

A call to the heliport had confirmed that my copter was scheduled to leave at four o'clock. During the flight back to the island, I decided that I would spend only enough time at Wiffen Cove to feed the cats and pick up a change of clothes. Then I would go back to the Sea Urchin Motel. I would not not spend another night alone in the House on Wiffen Cove.

Not that I intended to abandon my claim—I just wanted time to explore the place in the daylight, do some checking. Or something. Maybe, I thought, I should talk to the attorney. And Helen Riley would be moving in on Monday.

The flight back to the island under an overcast sky was uneventful; but just as I drove Stephen's car into the protection of the porte cochere, the sun broke through the clouds, blazing a golden path

across the waters of the strait, turning the small offshore island into a black shadow wreathed in radiance. And as I looked out over the water, suddenly,
midway between the two islands, a huge black and
white form broke the surface, rose straight up into
the air where it seemed to hang suspended, then
sank back into the water with scarcely a ripple. And
almost immediately another huge figure flashed upward, its magnificent body glistening. Only this second one rose in a graceful arc, up and over and
down in one long, lazy motion. I caught my breath
in admiration and awe. A pod of whales. A ballet of
the titans, so beautiful, so graceful for all their enormous size.

Quickly, I crossed the lawn to the top of the cove
stairs, all the while searching the waters for another
sighting. But they were gone. Now my gaze wandered down to the cove below. How calm and
peaceful it was. The tide was still flowing outward. I
looked for the rocks where Marsh and I had sat the
day he told me to beware of swimming alone, and I
began to tremble even before my brain acknowl-
edged what my eyes were seeing.

There, in a jumble of rocks and seaweed and
sand, huddled against the base of the boulder on
which Marsh had perched, was a body—a man—
lying face down in the ebbing tide.

# FOURTEEN

Numb with shock, I stared down at the body. For an interminable moment, I couldn't think, couldn't decide what I should do.

I gasped and my hands flew to my mouth as an incoming wave broke against the man's body, lifting it, causing it to rock gently, then settle more deeply into the sand, its movement a parody of life. But the man was dead. I knew he was dead. I also knew I had to notify someone.

I stumbled back to my car as quickly as I could and started to get in, intent on going for help. Then I thought, No, I can reach someone faster by telephone.

But the sun was already racing down the sky and it would soon be dark. Dear God, I thought. I can't go into that house alone! But I was already moving across the lawn. I had to call the police.

I followed the graveled path around to the back of the house to the servants' entrance. I unlocked the door and tiptoed in. My fingers found the switch on the wall to the left and flipped it, flooding the area with light.

I glanced about, mentally berating myself for having failed to get a telephone extension for the kitchen. But there was no turning back. Taking a deep breath, I hurried on, and the hollow echo of my footsteps, like a ghostly presence, followed me up the hall.

When I reached the phone, I snatched it up and signaled frantically for the operator.

When she answered, I said, "Please . . . send someone right away . . . there's a dead man on the beach."

"Who is this?" The operator's voice was calm, assured.

"Kimberly D'Ahl . . . at Wiffen Cove."

"Are you certain the man is dead?"

"Yes, yes! I'm positive. Please hurry."

"What is your address Ms. D'Ahl?"

"No address. It's the only house on Wiffen Cove. The sheriff will know . . . please, Operator, we're wasting time!"

"All right, Ms. D'Ahl; but please stay by your phone. The sheriff will want you to show him where the body is located."

I nodded my head and hung up the phone.

I returned to the hall and half ran back to the kitchen. Clarence and Cleo were sitting patiently by their dishes. They both stood up and began to prance when I entered. Sheba, who had been sleeping in one of the chairs, jumped down, stretched, and came to curl herself about my ankles.

It wasn't until I took off my coat and reached into the cupboard for the cat food that I remembered I was still wearing the dress in which I had left the house almost twenty-four hours before. Damn, damn, damn! I thought. I can't meet the sheriff dressed like this. And that meant I must go upstairs to change.

I walked out into the hall, climbed the stairs, and walked through the door into my room. There I stopped and stood staring, unable to believe what my eyes were telling me.

The clothes I had left on the foot of my bed were strewn across the floor in tatters. The articles I kept on my dressing table had been knocked to the floor, the more fragile items were smashed and their contents ground into the carpet. Even my bed had been savaged; the sheets and comforter stripped from the mattress and the sheets, like my clothing, torn and shredded.

Shocked, I walked straight into the room and began picking up my things. I was near the foot of the bed, bending down to retrieve a pillow, when that muffled whooshing noise I had heard only once before startled me. I jerked erect and spun about to face the sound.

Vera stood there, near the wardrobe, breathing heavily. Her hair was disheveled, covered with dust and cobwebs; her eyes, aglow with malevolence, stared at me, unblinking.

A thrill of fear shivered up my spine. "Vera?" My voice faltered.

Vera's hands clenched into fists. She took a step toward me. "You little bitch!" She spat the words at me.

I gazed at her in dismay.

"I warned you . . . I told you to leave." Her voice was cold and taut with barely controlled emotion.

"I don't understand. . . ." My voice sounded thin and reedy.

"Be still," she hissed. Her eyes narrowed as her gaze swept over me. "Look at you . . . tried to seduce Stephen, didn't you?"

"Stephen?" I echoed. I could make no sense of what she was saying; neither could I understand what she was doing in my room.

"Did he kiss you . . . touch you . . . make love to you?" Her mouth twisted as if the words had a bitter taste.

The anger and hatred emanating from Vera seemed to reach out and engulf me. I realized then that I had to get away from her and quickly. I let my eyes slide from Vera's face to the hall door and back. She did not miss the meaning in my glance. Her muscles tensed and she stood poised.

Vera was probably twenty years older than I. She was also taller and heavier, and I didn't doubt for one moment but that she was stronger; and although I was closer to the door than she, I knew that in a race, she would win.

"Please, Vera," I said, hoping to placate her, "I really don't understand."

"I don't understand." She mimicked my voice, then added in a strident, angry tone, "You don't need to understand . . . not now. It's too late!"

I tried another approach. "Vera, I've got to change my clothes . . . why don't you wait for me downstairs." As I spoke, I slipped off my coat and loosened the tie with which I had belted my skirt.

"Ha!" The sound exploded from between her teeth. Then she sneered, "Are you expecting someone? Stephen, perhaps?"

"Yes . . . no . . . I mean I'm expecting the sheriff. There's a body . . ."

She didn't give me time to finish. She moved so quickly, she had my wrist clasped in an iron grip and was dragging me across the room before the words left my mouth.

Caught off guard, I was unprepared to resist her sudden onslaught. As she jerked me forward, I lost one of my high-heeled slippers, tripped on the hem of my dress, and unable to regain my balance, fell to my knees. Vera didn't falter in her stride; she pulled me along behind her as easily as if I had been a king-size feather pillow.

She dragged me as far as the wall before she hoisted me back onto my feet. "Now, come along peacefully, or I'll break your arm!" she snarled. With a vicious wrench of my wrist, she made it perfectly clear that she not only could, she would carry out her threat if given provocation.

Maintaining her hold on me with one hand, she inserted the fingers of her other under the wainscoting just below the wall lamp. With a quiet swoosh, a portion of the paneling slid upward into the wall above revealing a steep narrow staircase festooned with cobwebs and thick with dust.

Vera jerked me around, then pushed me ahead of her into the opening. The air inside was chill and musty. A large hairy spider scuttled into a cocoon of dusty web only inches from my face.

Vera released my wrist and snapped, "Get down those stairs!"

Then I heard the panel slide shut once more and we were left in a murky half-light that filtered up from some invisible source below.

I hesitated, in such a state of shock I could scarcely comprehend what was happening to me.

"I said, 'down the stairs!' " Vera repeated, giving me a shove that sent me sprawling, and I might have tumbled all the way to the bottom had I not managed to grab onto the handrail. I lost the other slipper and my dress sustained another rip as I again stepped on the hem.

"Move!" At the sound of Vera's voice, I grabbed up my skirt and practically slid down the stairs.

From the bottom, a narrow curving tunnel led forward, sloping downward at a gentle angle. The floor and walls were of smooth, dry stone.

"Keep moving," Vera hissed. "I'll tell you when to stop."

When at last we reached the end of the tunnel, I saw that the light came from a floodlamp that hung above a heavy, rough-hewn door that blocked the exit.

When we reached it, Vera snapped, "Open the door . . . it's not locked." I grasped the handle, pulled, and it swung open, moving silently on well-oiled hinges.

We stepped through into a large, brightly lit chamber. It reminded me of nothing so much as a bank vault lined with safety deposit boxes. The air here was fresh, and the floor, beneath my stockinged feet, felt warm and clean. We did not stop. Vera urged me straight across the room to an exit in the opposite wall, pulled a set of keys from her pocket, and unlocked the door.

Another savage shove sent me staggering through. It seemed that the very act of administering physical abuse gratified Vera while at the same time fed her fury. And the effect, for me, though painful was also stimulating. It filled me with anger that offset the fear that had threatened to immobilize me. My mind was beginning to function, I was thinking, taking note of my surroundings.

The chamber in which we now stood resembled the first except that the walls to right and left each contained two large cages of the type used in most of the big zoos before 1950. Vera herded me into the one nearest at hand and clanged its iron bars shut behind me.

I whirled about and grabbed hold of the bars. "Vera! For God's sake . . . what do you think you are doing?" I shook the bars—or tried to. They were securely anchored top and bottom in steel reinforced concrete.

Vera stood back, her eyes gloating, her lips curled in a sardonic smile.

Suddenly, the fear in me gained the upper hand again, and I shrank back a step.

Sound, not unlike laughter, yet filled with evil, bubbled up in Vera's throat. Then she turned, walked quickly to a door on the far side of the room, and disappeared without a word.

I turned and glanced about the cage. It contained nothing. The floor was of cement. There was a covered drain in the center. Along the back wall, about waist-high, there was a sturdy wooden ledge.

I no longer felt anything—not even fear. My brain was numb. I couldn't think what to do. Slowly, my knees gave way beneath me and my hands slid down the bars as I sank into a crouch, then collapsed against the wall.

However, my eyes continued to explore my situation—I noted that on either side of the door through which Vera had departed, there were tall, white, enameled cabinets, the kind often used to store medical supplies. They were shaped like hutches. Through the glass doors in the top section, an array of bottles and jars as well as other medical supplies were visible. A metal work surface extended outward at about waist height, and beneath it was a set of metal doors. In the center of the room stood a large, metal-topped gurney with a high-power lamp suspended above it. There were no windows, neither could I locate any air vents.

I was still huddled on the floor when Vera returned. She came directly to me, shoved a damp washcloth and a comb through the bars, and said, "Get up! Wipe off your face and comb your hair."

Dumbfounded, I stared at her, trying to pull myself together.

She didn't wait. Reaching through the bars, she grabbed a handful of my hair and gave it a yank. "Get up! Wash your face and comb your hair."

Pain clawed at my scalp. I emitted a startled yelp and scuttled backward out of her reach, but I didn't stand up. "I won't," I mumbled.

"You will if you want to live. Believe me, it would give me great pleasure to dispose of you."

I raised my head and glared at her. "You wouldn't dare," I said, but the tremor in my voice belied my brave words.

She nodded over her shoulder toward the cabinets. "See those?" She laughed a short ugly laugh. "Everything I need is right there." She gave me a black look, then snapped. "Get up and wash your face . . . I won't tell you again," and she started to walk toward the cabinets.

Abruptly, my bravado deserted me. I scrambled to my feet. I hadn't the courage to call her bluff—if it were a bluff. Quickly, I scrubbed the dust and tear streaks from my face, ran the comb through my hair.

Vera smiled, acknowledging her victory. "Now get out there in the middle and stand still. I need some pictures." She reached in her pocket and pulled out a tiny camera. "Stand still," she ordered, and the camera clicked. "Now in profile," and again the camera clicked. "Face me again . . . I need a smile . . . now profile, hands behind your head."

Moving like a robot, I did exactly as I was bid.

Finally, her camera clicked for the last time, and she turned and left without a word. When Vera returned a few moments later, I had pulled myself up onto the wooden ledge and curled myself into a ball. She shoved a tray through a narrow slot in the bottom of the gate. That done, she turned and started for the exit once more.

I bolted upright and called after her, "Vera . . . please . . . wait. . . ." She didn't.

I slipped down from the ledge once more and went to get the tray. On it there was a bottle of water, a small carton of milk, a bowl of soup, and some bread and butter. Just the sight of the food seemed to revive me, start me thinking again.

I carried the tray back, deposited it on the ledge, and grabbed the milk carton. Then I stopped. Slowly, I put it down as I said softly, under my breath, "She can keep me in a cage like an animal, but she can't make me act like one."

Thereupon, I turned myself about, retrieved the washcloth from the spot where I had dropped it earlier, and redampened it with water from the bottle. Then I scrubbed off as much of the grime from my hands, arms, and shoulders as I could. Only then did I allow myself to wolf down the food.

The soup was lukewarm and greasy; the bread was stale. Nonetheless, I did feel better when I had eaten. Next, I turned my attention to my clothing. Without my high heels, the dress was at least two inches too long, and each time I stepped on the dragging skirt, it suffered new damage. I decided the best thing to do was to tear it off at knee length and use what I could salvage as a kind of wrap—or a pillow if I had to sleep on that wooden ledge.

I had barely finished shortening my costume when the lights began to dim, fading quickly into stygian darkness. Numb with exhaustion, too tired to think or care, I felt my way back to the ledge, climbed up, curled myself into a ball, and immediately fell into a deep sleep.

The clanging of the cage gate jarred me back to consciousness. I was cold and stiff and my body felt bruised from the hard surface on which I lay. When I tried to turn over, to stretch out, pain shot through my cramped hip and knee joints causing me to whimper softly.

"You'll live. . . ." The sound of Vera's voice brought all the events of the past few hours rushing back, and I sat up quickly despite the ache in my muscles.

"I've brought you some breakfast." She smiled,

but her eyes were cold. She was standing just outside the cage holding last night's empty tray in her
hands. Another tray sat on the floor just inside the
gate.

A tremor shivered through me, but I said nothing.

Vera walked over to the gurney, and with an agil-
ity and grace I had not suspected she possessed,
hoisted herself to a sitting position atop it.

But it wasn't a gurney! Suddenly I realized that it
was actually a surgical table, and another tremor
coursed through me. What kind of a place was this?

"Eat your breakfast," Vera commanded.

Obediently I retrieved the tray, carried it back to
the shelf, and began to eat. She had brought a serv-
ing-size box of cornflakes, milk, a couple of stale
sweet rolls, and a pot of tea. The tea, at least was hot
and strong. I curled my cold fingers around the cup
and breathed deep of the fragrant steam. Then I
added a bit of milk and drank it gratefully.

I ate slowly, all the while covertly observing Vera.
This morning she was again the carefully groomed
and well-tailored woman I had thought of as a
friend. But now her eyes, as she watched me, were
entirely impersonal and as cold as hoarfrost. She sat
primly, legs neatly crossed at the ankles, hands
folded together, palms up, in her lap.

When I had finished eating, she said, "I'm bring-
ing you some visitors a little later today." She
smiled, but the smile was not reassuring.

I took a deep breath, tried to steady my voice before I asked, "Why are you doing this, Vera? Where
are we? What do you want from me?"

She didn't answer immediately, and when she
did, she totally ignored my questions. Glancing

around the chamber, she observed, "You're very lucky, you know. In my grandfather's time this place was not so comfortable."

"Your grandfather . . . ?"

Vera sat a little straighter, lifted her chin a bit higher. "Yes, my grandfather. I was born in the House on Wiffen Cove . . . as was Stephen." When she mentioned Stephen, the ghost of a shadow flitted across her face and she became very still, all her attention suddenly turned inward.

When Vera remained silent, I tried again. "What is this place?"

Vera took a deep breath, looked at me in surprise, as if I should have known. "The stockroom, of course!"

"Stockroom . . . ?"

Ignoring my interruption, Vera continued, "In Grandfather's day, they just used the bare caves. They never held merchandise very long." She sighed. "Times change." Again she glanced around and her look was approving. "LeBeauforte did a good job. We can handle all kinds of merchandise now . . . and hold it indefinitely."

I could make no sense at all of what she was saying and I shifted uneasily on the wooden ledge.

The silence hung between us, thick and oppressive until Vera suddenly continued, "In Grandfather's day it was mostly whiskey and Chinamen. Beau was into paintings and drugs."

Smirking, she added, "They'd all be pleased if they could see how we've branched out . . . high-tech components, arms, exotic animals . . . if a client has the money, we can get him whatever he wants."

At the mention of animals, I stiffened.

Vera didn't miss a thing. "We had a snow leopard down here when you first arrived—noisy creature, but very profitable."

She paused, looked at me, and began to laugh. "If you could have seen yourself that first day; I've never seen anyone move quite so fast!"

Some of the pieces suddenly meshed inside my head—so that was what had made that fearful sound, and that was why I had so often felt that I was not alone in the house, that I was being watched.

Vera, as if she could read my mind, laughed again. "Have you finally figured it out? It was me, of course. I've been coming and going at will. I hoped moving things around, leaving doors open . . . why, just that trick with the ultra-high-frequency sound should have been enough to send you packing."

"Ultra . . . high . . . frequency?" I faltered.

"Of course. After Beau died, Sylvia wanted out of the business. When she realized the only way she'd make it was feet first, she had the place wired so that anyone climbing the stairs automatically tripped a high-frequency alarm that could be heard only by those Dobermans of hers. If that alarm sounded, those two dogs set up such a howling it would wake the dead. Waste of time and money, of course, with that underground entrance straight into the bedroom. I'm surprised Beau never told her about it."

More pieces fell into place. "That's what scared the cats!"

A cruel smile curled Vera's lips. "Right. They

could hear that UHF signal, too . . . spooked them good." Her laughter was malicious. "Put the fear of God into you, too, when those cats refused to come upstairs, didn't it?"

Slowly the smile faded from her face; she sighed, her shoulders drooped. "But you're a stupid, stubborn little bitch and that Special Agent you've got sniffing around . . ." Vera sighed. "We'll have to dispose of him, too."

I gasped as my mind made another connection. The dust and cobwebs in that stairwell behind the closet. Vera had been covered with them. . . . "You killed Aunt Sylvia!"

Vera stiffened and glared at me. Abruptly she relaxed and laughed deprecatingly. "Not exactly. It was an accident. Actually, I rather liked Sylvia. But she simply refused to mind her own business . . . made a real nuisance of herself with her threats and hysteria. So I put a dart in her one night to keep her out of the way while we were moving a big shipment. I never dreamed she'd wake up and . . ." Vera shrugged. "She should have done as she was told."

*A dart!* And dust left behind by whoever had put me in bed. "That's what you did to me, too!" I accused.

Vera laughed. "Works every time!"

"But how could you see? The room was pitch black that night."

Vera gave me a disgusted look. "Nightscope, of course—infrared light."

Sickened by her revelations, frightened, I finally forced myself to ask, "Why are you keeping me here?"

Vera looked at me and her smile was sardonic. "Tsk! Come now. Surely a woman of your wiles is smarter than that."

Exasperation overcame my fear and I snapped, "I don't know what you mean!"

"You thought you had Stephen wrapped around your little finger, didn't you?" she sneered. "Well, Stephen wasn't taken in. He wanted to dump you off the cliff instead of Marjory."

Her words were a flail to my senses, laying my nerves bare, but I tried not to let my feelings show in my face. Had Stephen wanted to kill me? Had he been the one who threw Marjory over the cliff? No, I told myself. It's not true! Vera's lying.

While these thoughts tormented me, Vera, lips pursed, was lost in thoughts of her own. When at last she spoke, it was in a conversational tone. "You know," she said, "after all the cash we put into her, that damned leopard died."

I finally understood and for the first time, a feeling akin to hate suffused me. Smuggling. Can there be anything more cruel, more reprehensible, than the illicit trade in endangered species? Like lava spewing from a volcano, my anger completely overrode all other feelings, and I shouted, "You'll pay for her death, Vera! I swear I'll see to it that you pay!"

She laughed merrily. "Oh, you will, will you?" The laughter stopped as abruptly as it began and she studied me through slitted lids. Then, musingly, "There's a tremendous market for red-haired, green-eyed women. We might recoup our losses yet. We'll have our money, and you . . ." She broke off in midsentence, her words replaced by laughter as she slid down from the table and walked out.

I jumped from the ledge and ran to the bars of the cage screaming, "Vera . . . Vera . . . come back. . . ."

There was no answer, not even an echo. I grabbed the bars and tried again to shake them. They remained absolutely solid. I continued to shout, but not for long. My hands dropped to my sides. I'm alone, I thought. This time I'm really all alone, and there is no one out here to hear me.

I went back to the ledge, climbed up, and sat cross-legged considering my situation. Vera's crazy, I thought. But that made her last statement even more horrifying. *A market for women!* Did she smuggle people as well as animals? Surely, she was only trying to frighten me. But why? I wondered. And why did she keep saying such awful things about me? Why did she hate me so much?

As for what she had said about Aunt Sylvia, I closed my mind against the memory. It was too awful. . . .

The lights began to dim. In sudden terror, I called out, "Please, Vera, please don't turn out the lights!"

But the light continued to fade until the room was in total, absolute darkness. I jerked my knees up against my chest and curled myself into a ball with my back pressed against the wall. The panic that last night's exhaustion had preempted now overpowered me. I felt as if I were drowning in the velvet-thick blackness. I couldn't breathe. I couldn't move. I couldn't even think.

Light, glowing blood-red through my eyelids, urged me back to wakefulness.

"Come on . . . get up." It was Vera's voice.

"Here, wash your face and comb your hair again."
She tossed a washcloth into the center of the cage.

I didn't move, didn't open my eyes.

Silence. Then the sound of Vera's footsteps retreating, metal doors opening, footsteps returning.
Silence.

Terrified, I opened my eyes. Vera stood just outside the cage with a gun in her hand.

"Now," she sighed, "you can cooperate, or I can
put a dart in you and leave you down on the
beach. . . ."

Once again, I had not the courage to defy her. I
scrambled down from the ledge, picked up the
washcloth, and scrubbed my face. Then I dragged
the comb through my hair.

When I had finished, Vera ordered, "Now stand
up straight . . . there in the middle." She held her
head to one side and observed me with a critical
eye, sighed. "Well, you look a little rough around the
edges, but with that body and that complexion . . .
we'll see."

My heart lurched, began to thud against my ribs.
Surely, she didn't mean . . .

While my imagination raced, Vera walked back to
the medical supply cabinet and put the gun away.
Then she returned to me. "Now, you do exactly as
you are told, and don't speak unless spoken to. Understand?"

Trembling, I nodded my head. I couldn't believe
this was really happening. It must be a nightmare, I
thought. Yes, that was it, a nightmare, and in a few
moments David would walk in and kiss me and say,
"Wake up sleepy-head. . . ."

I watched Vera leave to return almost immedi-

ately followed by two men. One was tall and thin
with fine slender features, an aquiline nose, and
piercing black eyes. His lips were thin and, I
thought, he could probably be cruel. He was smiling
at Vera and murmuring something too low for me to
hear. The other man was shorter and overweight.
His skin was pasty, his suit flashy, his eyes heavy-
lidded, and his face wore a perpetual smirk.

They stopped a few paces in front of the cage and
stared at me.

A cramp began to gather in my solar plexus.

After a pause, Vera ordered, "Walk for us, Ms.
D'Ahl . . . do some knee bends."

I obeyed.

The three of them held a whispered conversation.

Vera nodded, then snapped at me. "Put your
hands behind your head and turn around . . .
slower!"

Suddenly, shame and anger overcame the fear
that had held me prisoner, and I turned on Vera.
"No!" I shouted, "I won't! I'm not a . . . a . . . a
piece of merchandise." I whirled about, turning my
back on them, and retreated to the far side of the
cage.

They all laughed! One of the men said, "Bravo!
My client appreciates a woman with spirit."

"Have you seen enough? Are we ready to discuss
details?" That was Vera's voice.

The other man said, "No, I want to see what I'm
bidding on. Tell her to take off her clothes."

"Don't be vulgar!" That was Vera's voice again.
"I'll not stand here and watch you ogle a nude. It's
not decent!"

One of the men guffawed—an ugly sound. "Always the lady, eh, Vera?"

"Watch your tongue, Marvin!" There was ice in Vera's tone.

"But I want to know what I'm getting. Your brother Steve always . . ."

"Shut your foul mouth!" I had never heard such fury in another person's voice, and for a moment the room filled with absolute silence. Then Vera inquired in a perfectly natural tone, "Have we ever cheated you?"

At last the sound of retreating footsteps, and again I was alone.

I did not move. Anger, shame, and terror paralyzed me. I couldn't think what to do. The room began to grow dark and I did not know whether it was the light that was fading or my consciousness slipping away, and still I stood there, leaning against the shelf. I don't remember lying down.

A strong hand on my shoulder, shaking me, calling me back to the light, roused me. I opened my eyes. I was huddled on the floor, leaning against the wall under the wooden ledge. The tall, thin man who had been there earlier with Vera was bending over me. It was his hand that grasped my shoulder.

"Come, little one, it is time to go." His voice was mellow and his words were spoken with a barely perceptible accent.

I only stared at him and cowered closer to the wall.

"There is nothing to fear. Come and see, I have brought shoes and a coat for you." He made a quick, small gesture with his head and another man stepped forward, set a pair of soft felt slippers on the floor in front of me, then flung open a long dark cloak of some thick, supple material and displayed it over his arm for all the world like a salesperson in a fashionable boutique. It would have been funny had I not been so terrified.

"Come . . . I will help you." It was the dark man still speaking in that quiet voice. He slipped his hands under my arms and lifted me to my feet as easily as I lift Cleo. I didn't resist. I felt weak, drained, and my knees would not support me. When I began to sink toward the floor once more, the dark man caught me and set me on the ledge. Again he made that small, quick gesture with his head.

Instantly, the other man picked up the shoes and slipped them on my feet. Next, he swirled the cape about my shoulders, and then, with a movement so practiced I could scarcely follow it, he lifted me, slipped the tail of the garment under me, then zipped it up the front.

Only then did I realize that it was not exactly a cape; it more nearly resembled a sacque—similar to the kind you put on a baby, closed at the bottom and fitting snugly about the throat. I was perfectly free to move about within its folds; but I was as totally secured as I would have been had they tied me hand and foot.

From my position on the ledge, I could see Vera standing near the door between the medical supply cabinets. Her eyes were fixed on me with a baleful intensity that made me cringe, but I could not withdraw my eyes from hers. Even when the tall man picked me up and started across the room, her malevolent gaze followed.

As we brushed past her, I heard her whisper, "It's all your fault . . . you killed him. . . ."

In a dim, impersonal way I wondered how she knew about my guilt over David. Yes, David was dead, my baby was dead . . . but Vera, with all she had on her conscience, certainly had no right to accuse me. Still, it scarcely mattered now. Now the important thing was to escape!

*Escape*. Just thinking it was like a shot of adrenaline. The fatigue, the fear receded and my mind began to function clearly. Be ready, I told myself. Once we are outside . . .

Without warning, a blast of damp, cold air washed over my face. I opened my eyes. We were in the cove surrounded by several figures all dressed in tight-fitting dark suits. They were talking softly among themselves in a tongue I did not recognize.

Then I heard the shushing sound of something being dragged along the beach, and I began to struggle against the arms that held me. "Put me down . . . let me go," I shouted, thrashing about wildly inside the garment that confined me.

With one fluid motion, my captor let the lower portion of my body fall and thrust me from him, still maintaining a viselike grip on my shoulder. With his free hand, he struck me a stinging blow across the face, then pulled me close once more; and still his voice was gentle, mellow, as he murmured against my ear, "Be still." Then he scooped me up once more, and forced my face against his shoulder so deftly, so tightly, that I could barely breathe let alone see or cry out.

My lungs clamored for oxygen and consciousness was beginning to slip away when at last his grasp relaxed and he allowed my body to roll gently onto a soft yielding surface. With my face, my mouth and nose, freed of his shoulder, I gasped for air, then opened my eyes. I was rocking gently to and fro in the bottom of an inflatable raft.

The man slipped an arm under me and lifted me to a sitting position before he whispered against my ear, "Be quiet and you will be quite safe."

Now I could see clearly: the cove slipping away behind us; the waters of the strait, black and cold and deep, spread out about us.

Suddenly the night's stillness was rent by the roar of powerful engines. A brilliant light swept over us, moved on, hesitated, then moved slowly back to pinpoint our position.

My heart gave a great joyous leap of thanksgiving; but in the same instant, strong arms swept me up and dumped me over the side of the raft. I shrieked in abject terror as I slid down its smooth side and my mind exploded with horror.

I thrashed about wildly inside my shroud while all the horrors of the deep, all the pale and bloated obscenities that share a watery grave assaulted my mind. The frigid waters of the strait spread wide to receive me, its waves closed over my head, and I felt the searing torment of icy water agonizing my lungs.

# FIFTEEN

I was floating in the void—alone—in darkness. And for a time, I hovered there, looking down upon the shining waters of the Strait of Juan de Fuca. Calm and still and empty, they spread out below me, and I felt no regret. But even as I would have drawn away, a sudden blaze of light far below caught my attention.

Drifting nearer, I saw that it was a small ship, its searchlight fixed on something adrift on the surface of the water. A small wave washed over the object, and it began to sink.

Then I heard a splash, as someone dove over the ship's side. It scarcely mattered. It was already too late. . . .

Slowly, I began to float, to rise, up and up, higher and higher. I turned my head and watched, bemused, as I drifted, ever more quickly, toward a darkness gradually evolving within the night's darkness. And then I was within it, moving faster and faster toward a light that grew and grew until it was a blinding radiance; and the radiance was all around me, and within me, and part of me. And the radiance was pure love.

Then David was beside me, standing straight and

tall, and he took my hands in his. And I was filled with a joy that knew neither beginning nor end.

But David said, "You cannot stay."

I stared at him, speechless, and he knew my thoughts.

"You still have much to do," he said. And though he did not speak again, I knew he wanted me to be whole, without thought of guilt or sorrow; to return to Marshall Thorne, to life, to a family yet to be born.

I tried to plead with David, to tell him how happy I was to be with him once more, how I longed to stay; but I felt myself begin to float away, backward, and I was in the tunnel of darkness once more, and the light grew fainter and fainter and ever farther away. . . .

# SIXTEEN

Long before I opened my eyes, I knew I was in a hospital. The sheets that held me were as smooth as glass; and the silence that surrounded me was complete except for the occasional distant rustle of starched skirts, the squeak of crepe-soled shoes on polished floors. I knew, too, that there were flowers —roses, I thought—and, when finally I opened my eyes, they were there. Long-stemmed yellow roses in a crystal vase.

Late afternoon sunlight streamed through the window, casting the corners in darkness, and I did not see Marshall until he stood up, stepped forward, came to stand at the foot of my bed.

"How do you feel?" His voice was husky.

At the sight of him, I felt a sudden rush of happiness. "I'm so glad you're here," I whispered, and I patted the bed covers, urging him to sit beside me.

In an instant, he had circled the bed, perched himself carefully on the edge. Only then did I note how tired, how sad he looked. Fatigue lines were etched into the corners of his mouth, and his dark, gentle eyes were underscored by smudges of violet. His solemn gaze was intent upon my face.

"You're sure you're all right?"

I nodded. My throat felt rough and scratchy, and my chest hurt, but I was at peace. Had not David himself set me free? Never again would I struggle with that crushing load of guilt. I was ready to begin life anew. I had to tell Marsh, make him understand. There was so much to explain . . . but I knew everything would be all right. David would not have sent me back unless . . .

Abruptly, Marsh took my hands in his, leaned close to kiss my forehead as if I were a child.

In response, a tiny glow of warmth blossomed inside me and I slipped one hand free of his grasp, laid my fingers along his cheek.

Quickly he turned his head and left a kiss in my palm before asking, "Do you remember what happened?"

A tremor shuddered through me. "Yes," I whispered, "I remember . . . I know it was you who pulled me from the water. . . ."

Obviously startled by my statement, Marsh said, "You know. . . ."

I nodded. "You could have drowned . . . diving into that icy water. . . ."

An odd expression gathered behind Marsh's eyes, but he only said, "We'd have never found you if that *bag* you were in hadn't kept you afloat. It was made from a tightly woven woolen material that was practically impervious to water. The air trapped inside kept you from sinking. At least long enough for us to find you. . . ."

Suddenly the terror I had felt as I was tossed over the side of that little boat, the memory of the icy water knifing into my lungs, set me to trembling.

Marsh pulled me into his arms, held me close,

comforted me, and when I was calm once more he whispered, "Thank God you are safe . . . we thought for a while we'd lost you. . . ."

Without thinking, I murmured, "It was David sent me back."

Marsh's embrace tightened, then slowly he released me, settled me back against the pillow. Though he said nothing, I knew he understood, and for a while we remained silent, fingers entwined, content to be alive, to be together.

But there was so much I needed to know. Hesitantly I put the question to Marsh.

"Don't worry about it now," he said. "It's over. We'll talk about it when you are on your feet once more."

I didn't push.

We both smiled at the nurse when she opened the door and switched on the light. She smiled, too.

Despite my objections, the doctor insisted on keeping me in the hospital overnight. Actually, I was glad he did. Once Marsh had assured me that Helen Riley was taking care of Sheba, Cleo, and Clarence; that the police had Vera and the men from the raft safely behind bars; I slept serenely through the night.

Marsh checked me out of the hospital early the following morning and drove me back to Wiffen Cove. Helen Riley met us at the door, led the way to the back parlor where she had a fire blazing merrily on the hearth and the three cats waiting to greet me.

Marsh made me sit down on the sofa, and he spread an afghan over my knees before he eased himself down beside me. Sheba jumped up, squeezed herself between us, and burst into song.

Helen brought us a pot of herbal tea and some
sticky buns, fresh from the oven, fragrant with cinnamon and cloves.

"Did you really bake these from scratch?" I was
openmouthed with admiration.

Helen smiled. When she had gone, we gave each
of the cats a saucer of milk, then ate the rolls, licked
the gooey icing from our fingers, and spoke in
monosyllables of inconsequential things.

It was I who brought up the subject we had both
been avoiding. "Stephen's dead, isn't he?" I said the
words calmly, surprised that I felt so detached, as if
the recent past had been a story I had read, not
something I had lived.

Marsh's gaze left the fire, fixed upon my face. At
last he nodded. "I'm sorry," he said.

"I saw the body . . . him . . . down in the cove.
I didn't know who it was . . . then. But just before
those men took me down to the cove, Vera said, 'It's
your fault he's dead.' I thought she meant David.
But I suddenly realized last night that she couldn't
have known about that. So she must have meant
Stephen. . . ."

Marshall nodded. After a moment's silence, he
asked, "Do you want to talk about it?"

I considered his question, tried to analyze my feelings, tried to organize my thoughts. Sooner or later,
I would have to confront the past. I decided sooner
was better. "Yes. . . ."

Abruptly, Marshall stood up, walked to the window, stood staring out, hands clasped behind his
back. "Perhaps you should begin by telling me everything you know. . . ."

I thought for a minute, then ventured, "I guess I

don't really know that much. Vera did say that she and Stephen were born in this house. Was that true?"

"Yes, the house was built by their grandfather, Hiram Enders Croft. He had one son, Daniel."

"But Stephen told me the old man was a bachelor. . . ."

Marsh shook his head. "Don't know why he would have said that unless he wanted to be certain you wouldn't suspect that he and Vera had been connected to the house."

Marsh fell silent and we both remained lost in thought for a moment. Then he continued, "Daniel never amounted to much . . . married a local girl and had the two children, Vera and Stephen. They always claimed that the old man struck it rich in the Klondike. The truth is, he was involved in many ventures, the chief of which was smuggling."

I nodded. "Vera told me that place where she had me was the stockroom."

"Right. No one knows how the old man discovered those caves; but he obviously understood their potential, especially after he realized the entrance from the strait is below water level except at low tide.

"He built this house about 1860; then he constructed that entrance between the caves and the bedroom for his own private use. There's another passage that leads from the caverns up to the old carriage house; it was used for business purposes. He dealt mostly in contraband whiskey and Asian aliens."

At his words, a shudder rippled through me. "Is

that who you were talking about that day at Deadman's Cove?''

Marsh turned to look at me. "He wasn't the only one, not even the first involved. But, yes." He paused, then continued, "I thought you might already know. . . ."

"How would I know?"

Marshall shrugged, turned back to the window.

So I asked, "And the property remained in the family until after Stephen and Vera were born?"

"Yep. Stephen was three and Vera thirteen when LeBeauforte bought the place for back taxes. That was in 1962."

Suddenly suspicious, I asked, "How do you happen to know all these details?"

"I'm with the Treasury Department."

I stared at his back while my mind raced. "Then you're the Special Agent Vera said was 'sniffing' around!"

Marsh stiffened, turned to face me. "She said that . . . a Special Agent was sniffing around?"

Ignoring his question, I continued, "You've been working on this case from that very first day! That's why you told me that silly story about wanting to buy the house. But why didn't you just tell me all this right from the beginning?"

For a long moment, Marsh gazed at me. Then he strode back to the sofa and sank down beside me. "I wanted to . . . from that very first afternoon; but I had to conduct the investigation according to certain rules."

I could only shake my head. "I don't understand."

"Well, until the case was solved, everyone was suspect. . . ."

Dismay swept over me. "You mean you really thought I might somehow be mixed up with all . . . this?"

"Of course not!" he declared hotly. Then, slowly, his expression underwent a subtle change and his eyes begged me to understand as he admitted, "That's not entirely true. In the beginning, I really wasn't sure, and a lot of lives besides my own were at stake."

He took a deep breath, ran his fingers through his hair. "Please try to understand, Kim. I learned the hard way that just because a beautiful woman has an angelic smile and trusting eyes, it does not necessarily follow that she is an all-American girl. . . ."

His own eyes had turned stormy. Abruptly he stood up, went to put another log on the fire. Sheba, wakened from her nap, jumped down and stalked off, grumbling quietly to herself. Marsh returned and sat down beside me once more.

I reached out, touched his hand, said softly, "It's all right, Marsh, I really do understand."

He took me in his arms then, and I turned to snuggle close against his chest, my head resting on his shoulder. I could feel his heart, its beat strong beneath my breast. How safe I felt, how full of peace. . . .

But at last we drew apart and I said, "Now, tell me the rest, please," and Marsh continued.

"After old man Croft died, Daniel and his family lived off the inheritance. Daniel either lacked the talent or the stomach for the family business. Whatever, by the time Vera and Stephen were born, everything of value had been sold. Daniel committed suicide in 1960 leaving his wife with the two kids and no visible means of support."

"But they did continue to live here?"

"For a while. How Dan's wife managed to hang on to the property for as long as she did is a miracle. However, ultimately, the property was sold for back taxes."

I nodded. "That was when LeBeauforte bought the place. . . ."

"Um hum. I don't know for certain that LeBeauforte knew about the caves, but it seems likely. During the war, he was involved with an espionage ring that operated out of Las Vegas. That was where he found Sylvia."

Again I nodded. "David told me she ran away from home when she was in her teens . . . the family black sheep."

Marshall sighed. "Poor Sylvia. I think she really loved that heel LeBeauforte . . . he could be so charming. . . . By the time she found out what was going on, she was in too deep to get out . . . or he had convinced her she was."

Marsh's eyes filled with a gentle sadness. "I wish I could have helped her . . . she was always very kind to me."

Impulsively, I leaned near and brushed a kiss across his cheek. "I'm sure you did help just by being her friend. You were someone she knew she could trust. It probably meant a lot to her."

Marsh shrugged. LeBeauforte was a very smooth operator and the war ended before they were able to pin anything on him. He just dropped out of sight for a couple of years, then turned up here on the island. We knew a lot of the loot collected by the

Nazis was being siphoned through here . . . but we could never figure out exactly how until now."

"How long have you been on the case?"

"Not long, actually. When an ongoing investigation into the traffic in smuggled goods in this area pointed to Saturday Island as the most likely point of entry, I was brought into the case because I had lived on the island as a child. Once here, it didn't take me long to figure out that Vera and Stephen were involved."

"Didn't you remember them from when you were children?"

Now Marsh laughed. "No, I'm not quite that old. Besides, my family moved to the mainland about the time LeBeauforte died. With the change of names, it took me a while to figure out who they really were. They probably dropped the family name for just that reason. Anyway, Stephen lost no time in becoming friends with LeBeauforte and ingratiating himself with Sylvia. LeBeauforte's record went back a long way, and because of him, Sylvia, too, was suspect; but, as I said, from everything I've learned, I think Sylvia was always a pawn in LeBeauforte's, and later in Stephen and Vera's, machinations."

"Thank you for that," I said. "I'm glad you think Aunt Sylvia was innocent. I never met her, but somehow I've come to think of her with great affection. . . ."

Marsh smiled and patted my hand before he continued, "Three things seem pretty clear. First, Stephen and Vera wanted this place back. It had been in the family for more than a hundred years, and, as far as they were concerned, the state had no right to sell it.

"Second, Vera was only seventeen when their mother died. Vera assumed responsibility for Stephen. She seemed to have given up whatever chances she may have had for a life of her own and devoted herself to her baby brother."

"Seventeen!" I was aghast. "Why, at that age, she was only a child herself. How did she manage?"

"Events are pretty well documented. She took a daytime job as a waitress and went to school evenings. She had a real estate license by the time she was twenty-one. She's a hard worker and eventually she got her broker's license. Then came the real estate boom and she made a lot of money . . . all of which she spent on her baby brother. She fed him, clothed him, sent him to the best schools. Interviews with those who knew them confirm that nothing was too good for Vera's little brother Stephen. She spoiled him rotten, and she never let him forget that their one goal in life was to regain possession of the House on Wiffen Cove."

I nodded. "I guess I can understand that. But I can't understand why Vera sent me that note, why she tried to scare me away. Even if I hadn't taken possession of the place, it would not have been available. According to Sylvia's will, it would have reverted to the townspeople to be used for their benefit."

Marshall sat silent for a moment, collecting his thoughts before explaining. "At the outset, Vera's plans were not well thought out. She seems to have had the idea that if they could keep the place empty, they could continue their smuggling operations without any fear of discovery while at the same time exerting their influence in town to make Sylvia's will act to their, the Enderses', advantage. I think Vera even thought it might be possible to break the will."

Suddenly Marsh hugged me tight and there was a catch in his voice as he added, "But you didn't let that note scare you away!"

We gazed into each other's eyes for a long moment, secure in our love, filled with gratitude that we were safely together. But there were things I still did not understand, things I had to know. Tentatively, I continued.

"But once I was here, by marrying me Stephen would have automatically regained control. So I still don't understand why she hated me . . . why she . . ." My voice threatened to fail me, and I fell silent.

But Marshall understood. He pulled me close once more, then continued. "I don't believe it was really you . . . it was Stephen. From what Vera has said, though she's not too coherent right now, it seems that because she had given up so much for him, she expected him to devote his life to her. Nevertheless, with the understanding that you were to be disposed of as soon after the wedding as possible, she would have agreed to the marriage. But Stephen made the mistake of telling her he really loved you. That was more than Vera could endure. You see, once Stephen decided he was serious about you, not only were you taking him away from her, you stood in the way of her ever becoming mistress of the House on Wiffen Cove."

"But if Stephen and I had married, it would have been perfectly natural for him to bring his sister here to live with us."

"Ah, yes. But you would have been mistress. Vera would have lived here only on sufferance. That was not for her. She wanted things as they had been in her grandfather's day. She wanted the house, she wanted to be mistress of the house, and she wanted all of Stephen's attention.

"So she reverted to her original plan. Get rid of you and keep the place empty as long as possible. I guess she figured that as long as the house belonged to everyone, so to speak, it didn't really belong to anyone, and there was always the chance that they could break that will. But she didn't realize how strong Stephen's feelings for you really were. . . ."

Without warning, memories of that last night with Stephen filled my mind and I could feel the hot color rising in my cheeks. How much, I wondered, did Marshall know about that? I knew I would have to tell him someday, but not now. Instead, I said, "But surely . . . there must have been other women in Stephen's life. . . ."

Marsh gave a short harsh bark of laughter. "Many . . . but he never really cared about them. He used women . . . women like Marjory Blake—"

Startled, I interrupted. "What about Marjory Blake?"

Slowly, Marshall drew away from me, and when his eyes met mine, they were filled with pity. A knot of ice formed in my chest.

Finally, Marshall asked, "Sure you want to know?"

I didn't want to know! I wanted to flee, to forget I had ever known Stephen, ever heard of Marjory Blake. That was impossible of course, so I nodded.

"I've got to know. It's the only way I'll ever be able to put it all behind me."

"Well, the night you and Stephen ran into Marjory and Ted on the stairs there at Madelinne House, Marjory said something that Stephen didn't like."

I bowed my head, stared at my fingers twisting in my lap. I had known all along what Marjory meant—why had I lied to myself—pretended I didn't understand?

Suddenly Marsh stood up and began to pace back and forth. "Marjory was a good kid until she got mixed up with Stephen. She was smart, too, and when she realized he was getting tired of her, she found ways to make herself useful. She knew all too well what happened to Stephen's old girlfriends."

I forced myself to raise my head, look at Marshall. "You mean they sold them to Vera's friends. . . ."

"Either that, or local prostitution rings."

"Didn't people wonder what happened to them? I mean, if all Stephen's girlfriends disappeared . . ."

"Most of his girlfriends were not the sort that people worried about. You and Marjory seem to be exceptions."

I shuddered. "And Stephen killed her, afraid she'd tell me?"

Marsh stopped his pacing and looked at me. "It wasn't your fault!"

"I know," I said, "but how could I have been so gullible? It hurts. Poor Marjory." I sighed.

Marsh sat down again, and again put his arm about me. "I should have told you," he whispered against my ear. "I should have trusted my heart and you."

Again, I would have preferred to remain locked in

his embrace, but I forced myself to draw away. "Tell me the rest," I said.

Marsh sighed, then continued. "According to Teddy, after Stephen left you, he telephoned Teddy and told him to bring Marjory out to the parking lot. Stephen met them there and the two men took her to Wiffen Cove."

"But why would Teddy do such a thing?"

"He was Vera's gofer. When either Vera or Stephen spoke, Teddy jumped. It was Teddy who actually killed Marjory. Vera pointed the finger in his direction when we picked her up, and Ted finally admitted his part in the business."

"They gave her a shot, then left her down on the beach," I whispered through lips numb with horror.

Marsh glanced at me, surprised. "How do you know?"

"That's what Vera threatened to do with me if I . . ."

Marshall didn't let me finish. He suddenly took me in his arms and held me close. "If that woman had hurt you . . ."

"She didn't . . . not really." Abruptly I drew away from Marshall as a monstrous thought began to form in my mind. My voice trembled as I whispered, "What happened to Stephen? I know he's . . . dead, but how . . . ?"

Marshall shook his head sadly. "Vera killed him."

"But why? How?"

"I could almost feel sorry for her if I didn't know how many lives she has ruined." Marsh drew a long breath, let it out slowly before continuing. "They had both been out of town for over a week. When Vera got back and found out that Stephen was with you, she flew into a rage. Apparently she called him, demanded he leave you and meet with her immediately. When they got here, Stephen reaffirmed his decision to marry you.

"Vera doesn't seem to remember exactly what happened next. Maybe she actually hit him with something, maybe he just stumbled. Anyway, he fell down the face of the cliff. He was dead before the tide ever reached him. . . ."

For a moment, I thought I was going to be sick. But I took a deep breath, then asked, "But why did she keep saying it was my fault?"

Marshall sighed. "Vera blames you for Stephen's death because, according to her, you made him fall in love with you. The twisted reasoning of a twisted mind."

We were each silent for a while, each lost in somber thoughts. Finally I asked, "And those men . . . the ones who were taking me away?"

"A bad lot! We're not certain exactly who they are. They aren't talking; but it's a pretty sure bet they're involved in procurement . . . whether for brothels, snuff films, or private harems, we haven't determined. But we'll nail them. Of that, you can be certain."

As I listened to Marsh, that shameful scene in the underground cage—the men staring at me—came rushing back into my mind and I suddenly felt sick.

Marsh, sensing my distress, said, "I shouldn't be telling you this. . . ."

"But I have to know. . . ."

"You're sure?"

"I'm sure."

"O.K." Marsh nodded. "It's a well-organized

business: women, young girls, and boys . . . even small children. They disappear every day."

I felt tears of sorrow and rage and frustration start in my eyes. Just to know such terrible things can happen—to have come so close to such a fate myself—was unnerving. I wanted to stop right there and forget everything that had happened. But there was one more question I had to ask.

Steeling myself, I pulled away from Marsh, stood up, went to stand before the fire. My throat felt tight, making it difficult to breathe. I swallowed, took a deep breath, finally managed to ask, "You do know that I was with Stephen?"

"I know," he said, and his voice was full of strain.

"I didn't love him," I said. "And nothing . . . happened . . . that night. But I needed somebody to want me. And he was always there for me . . . always thoughtful and generous . . . and I was so lonely. . . ."

Suddenly, Marshall was standing beside me. "It's all right. You don't have to explain . . . especially to me. I can't pretend it doesn't hurt, but if I hadn't put my job ahead of everything . . . My God! It's my fault you were ever in such danger."

I turned to look up at him. Our eyes met, and there was no more need for words.

"Oh, Marsh," I whispered, "hold me . . . hold me."

And he did.

# Epilogue

The House on Wiffen Cove has been turned into a combination gallery and teaching center for the arts. Each year at Christmastime, the foundation that was created to manage the project sponsors a beaux arts ball to raise money for scholarships. It is held in that lovely, third-floor ballroom. Both Rosemary, the girl who runs the art store, and Helen Riley are actively involved in the project.

As for the trust fund money I spent, since most of it went to clean and refurbish the house, the attorney was able to charge it back to the estate. Therefore, I did not have to make it good out of my own funds.

Vera was committed to an asylum for the criminally insane; she'll be there for the rest of her life. Teddy was sent to prison without hope of parole as was Marvin, the purveyor of porno and snuff films. The man who purchased me for his master, together with the other men in the raft that was carrying me out to their yacht, will serve at least twenty years. They will then be returned to their homeland.

Marsh and I were married that spring, and the two of us, together with my three cats and his two dogs, moved into a lovely old house on Whidbey Island. Marsh has given up his job with the government and is writing a book. I am still painting animal portraits. Our twins, David and Sylvia, will be four in May.